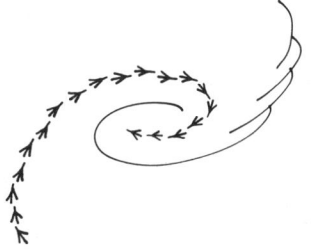

URSULA K. LeGUIN

The Visionary:
The Life Story of Flicker of the Serpentine

CAPRA PRESS
1984

Copyright ©1984 by Ursula Le Guin and Scott R. Sanders.
All rights reserved.
Printed in the United States of America.

Gratitude to the National Endowment for the Arts for their valuable assistance.

LIBRARY OF CONGRESS CATALOGING IN PUBLICATION DATA
Le Guin, Ursula K., 1929
THE VISIONARY.
No collective t.p. Titles transcribed from individual title pages.
Texts bound together back to back and inverted.
1. American fiction—20th century.
2. Audubon, John James, 1785-1851—Fiction.
I. Sanders, Scott R. (Scott Russell), 1945- . Wonders Hidden. 1984.
II. Title.   III. Title: Wonders hidden.
PS659.L4   1984   813'.54'08   84-7656
ISBN 0-88496-219-9 (pbk.)

PUBLISHED BY
Capra Press
Post Office Box 2068
Santa Barbara, California 93120

THE VISIONARY *is one of several autobiographies in a book called* Always Coming Home *(not yet published as I write this introduction). In the book are stories, life stories, histories, poems, and dramatic works of a people called the Kesh or the Valley People, who might be going to have lived in a particular region of Northern California a long time from now, as well as descriptions of their ways, pictures of their world, and examples of their music. In reading* THE VISIONARY, *it might be useful to know that Flicker's people are literate and non-industrial, with a stable technology adequate to their needs; that the Valley of the Na, its nine towns, and its beasts, birds, and plants are "the world" to Flicker and her townsfolk—a world perceived sacredly as nine Houses, five of which, named for the rocks Obsidian and Serpentine and the earths Blue Clay and Red and Yellow Adobe, form the principal institutions of society; and that these people differ from us most notably in their numbers, there being a couple of thousand of them in all, and the human population of the earth—according to the Exchange, a network of intelligent machines pursuing an evolutionary course separate from that of humanity—being a few hundred million all told (as before the rise of what we call Civilization).*

The Serpentine heyimas in Flicker's town, Telina-na, and

the Archives in Wakwaha-na, both had copies of her life story. It is probable that she was asked to write it as a kind of guide for other people burdened with her gift, for in it she tries to describe what was more often left unstated, the emotions and relationships of a person pursuing (willingly or unwillingly?) the career of visionary, and the place of a "great vision" in an ordinary life.

There are a few notes at the end to explain unfamiliar words or usages.

—UKL V 84

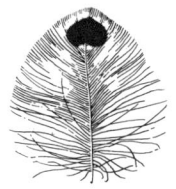

My mother and aunt said

that when I was learning to talk I talked to people they could not see or hear, sometimes speaking in our language and sometimes saying words or names they did not know. I can't remember doing that, but I remember that I could not understand why people said that a room was empty, or that there was nobody in the gardens, because there were always people of different kinds, everywhere. Mostly they stayed quietly, or were going about their doings, or passing through. I had already learned that nobody talked to them, and that they did not often pay heed or answer when I tried to talk to them; but it had not occurred to me that other people did not see them.

I had a big argument with my cousin once when she said there was nobody in the wash house, and I had seen a whole group of people there, passing things from hand to hand and laughing silently, as if they were playing some gambling game. My cousin, who was older than I, said I was lying, and I began to scream and tried to knock her down. I can feel that same anger now. I was telling what I had seen, and could not believe she had not seen the people in the wash house; I thought she was lying in order to call me a liar. That anger and shame stayed a long time, and made me unwilling to look at the people that other people didn't see, or wouldn't talk about. When I saw them, I looked away until they were gone. I had thought they were all my kinfolk, people of my household, and seeing them had been companionship and pleasure to me; but now I felt I could not trust them, since they had got me into trouble. Of course I had it all backwards, but there was nobody to help me get it straight. My family were not much given to thinking about things, and except for going to school I went to our heyimas only in the Summer before the games.

When I turned away from all those people that I had used to see, they went on, and did not come back. Only a few were left, and I was lonely.

I liked to be with my father, Olive of the Yellow Adobe, a man who talked little and was cautious and gentle in mind and hand. He repaired and re-installed solar panels and collectors and batteries and lines and fixtures in houses and outbuildings; all his work was with the Miller's Art. He did not mind if I came along if I was quiet, and so I went with him to be away from our noisy, busy household. When he saw that I liked his art he began to teach it to me. My mothers were not enthusiastic about that. My Serpentine grandmother did not like having a Miller for son-in-law, and my mother wanted me to learn medicine. "If she has the third eye she ought to put it to good use," they said, and they sent me to the Doctors Lodge on White Sulphur Creek to learn. Although I learned a good deal there, and liked the teachers, I did not like the work, and was impatient with the illnesses and accidents of mortality, preferring the dangerous, dancing energies my father worked with. I could often see the electrical current, and there were excitements of feeling, tones of a kind of sweet music barely to be heard, and tones also of voices speaking and singing, distant and hard to understand, that came when I worked with the batteries and wires. I did not speak of this to my father. If he felt and heard any of these things, he preferred to leave them unspoken, outside the house of words.

My childhood was like everybody's, except that with going to the Doctors Lodge and working with my father and liking to be alone, perhaps I played less with other children than many children do, after I was seven or eight years old. Also, though I went all over Telina with my father and knew all the ways and houses, we never went out of town. My family had no summer house and never even visited the hills. "Why leave Telina?" my grandmother would say. "Everything is here!" And in summer the town was pleasant, even when it was hot; so many people were away that there was never a crowd at the wash house, and houses standing empty were entirely different from houses full of people, and the ways and gardens and common places were lonesome and lazy and quiet. It was always in summer, often in the great heat of the afternoon, that I would see the people passing through Telina-na, coming upriver. They are hard to describe, and I have no idea who they were. They were rather short and walked quietly, alone, or three or four one after the other; their limbs were smooth and their faces round, often with some lines or marks drawn on the lips or chin; their eyes were narrow, and sometimes looked swollen and sore as if from smoke or weeping. They would go quietly through the town not looking at it and never speaking, going upriver. When I saw them I would always say the four heyas. The way they went, silently, gripped at my heart. They were far from me, walking in sorrow.

When I was nearly twelve years old my cousin came of age, and the family gave a very big passage party for her, giving away all kinds of things I didn't even know we had. The following year I came of age, and we had another big party, though without such lavishness, as we didn't have so much left to give. I had entered the Blood Lodge just before the Moon, and the party for me was during the Summer Dance. At the end of the party there were horse games and races, for the Summer people had come down from Chukulmas.

I had never been on horseback. The boys and girls who rode in the games and races for Telina brought a steady mare for me to ride, and boosted me up to her back and put the rein in my hand, and off we went. I felt like the wild swan. That was pure joy. And I could share it with the other young people; we were all joined by the good feeling of the party, and the excitement of the games and races, and the beauty and passion of the horses, who thought it was all their festival. The mare taught me how to ride that day, and I was on horseback all night dreaming, and the next day rode again; and on the third day I rode in a race, on a roan colt from a household in Chukulmas. The colt ran second in the big race when I rode him, and ran first in the match race when the boy who had raised him rode him. In all that glory of festival and riding and racing and friendship, I left my childhood most joyously, but also I went out of my House, and got lost from too much being given me at once. I gave my heart to the red colt I rode and to the boy who rode him, a brother of the Serpentine of Chukulmas.

It was a long time ago, and not his fault or doing; he did not know it. The word I write is my word; to myself let it be brought back.

So the Summer games were over in our town and the horse-riders went off downriver to Madidinou and Ounmalin; and there I was, a thirteen-year-old woman, and afoot.

I wore the undyed clothing I had been making all the year before, and I went often to the Blood Lodge, learning the songs and mysteries. Young people who had been friendly to me at the games remained friends, and when they found I longed to ride, they shared the horses of their households with me. I learned to play vetulou, and helped with caring for the horses, who were stabled and pastured then northwest of Moon Creek in Halfhoof Pasture and on Butt Hill. I said at the Doctors Lodge that I wanted to learn horse doctoring, and so they sent me to learn that art by working with an old man, Striffen, who was a great doctor of horses and cattle. He talked with them. It was no wonder he could heal them. I would listen to him. He used different kinds of noises, words like the matrix words of songs, and different kinds of silences and breathing; and so did the animals; but I never could understand what they were saying.

He told me once, "I'm going to die next year around Grass time."

I said, "How do you know that?"

He said, "An ox told me. He saw this. See?" He showed me that when he held out both his arms rigid, they had the sideways shaking or tremor of sevai.

"The later it begins the longer you live with it," said I, as I had learned at the Doctors Lodge; but he said, "One more World, one more Wine, the ox told me."

Another time I asked the old man, "How can I heal horses if I can't talk with them?" It seemed I was not learning much from him.

"You can't," he said. "Not the way I can. What are you here for?"

I laughed and shouted, like the man in the play,

> "What am I here for?
> What was I born for?
> Answer me! Answer!"

I was crazy. I was lost without knowing it, and did not care for anything.

Once when I came to the Obsidian heyimas for a Blood Lodge singing, a woman, I thought her old then, named Milk, met me in the passage. She looked at me with eyes as sharp and blind as a snake's eyes and said, "What are you here for?"

I answered her, "For the singing," and hurried by, but I knew that was not what she had asked.

In the Summer I went with the dancers and riders of Telina to Chukulmas. There I met that boy, that young man. We talked about the roan horse and about the little moon-horse I was riding in the vetulou games. When he stroked the roan horse's flank I did so too, and the side of my hand touched the side of his hand once.

Then there was another year until the Summer games returned. That was how it was to me: there was nothing I cared for or was mindful of but the Summer and the games.

The old horse-doctor died on the first night of the Grass. I had gone to the Lodge Rejoining and learned the songs; I sang them for him. After he was burned I gave up learning his art. I could not talk with the animals, or with any other people. I saw nothing clearly and listened to no one. I went back to working with my father, and I rode and looked after the horses and practiced vetulou so that I could ride in the games in Summer. My cousin had a group of friends, girls who talked and played soulbone and dice, gambling for candy and almonds, sometimes for rings and earrings, and I hung around with them every evening. There were no real people in the world I saw at that time. All rooms were empty. Nobody was in the common places and gardens of Telina. Nobody walked upriver grieving.

When the sun turned south the dancers and riders came again from Chukulmas to Telina, and I rode in the games and races, spending all day and night at the fields. People said, "That girl is in love with the roan stallion from Chukulmas," and teased me about it, but not shamefully; everybody knows how adolescents fall in love with horses, and songs have been made about that love. But the horse knew what was wrong: he would no longer let me handle him.

In a few days the riders went on to Madidinou, and I stayed behind.

Things are very obstinate and stubborn, but also there is a sweet willingness in them: they offer what they meet. Electricity is like horses: crazy and wilful, and also willing and reliable. If you are careless and running counter, a horse or a live wire is a contrary and perilous thing. I burnt and shocked myself several times that year, and once I started a fire in the walls of a house by making a bad connection and not grounding the wires. They smelled the smoke and put out the fire before it did much harm, but my father, who had brought me into his Art as a novice, was so alarmed and angry that he forbade me to work with him until the next rainy season.

At the Wine that year I was fifteen years old. I got drunk for the first time. I went around town shouting and talking to people nobody else saw: so I was told next day, but I could not remember anything of it. I thought if I got drunk again, but a little less drunk, I might see the kind of people I used to see, when the ways were full of them and they kept my soul company. So I stole wine from our house-neighbors, who had most of a barrel left in bottle after the dance, and I went down alone by the Na in the willow flats to drink it.

I drank the first bottle and made some songs, then I spilled most of the second bottle, and went home, and felt sick for a couple of days. I stole wine again, and this time I drank two bottles quickly. I made no songs. I felt dizzy and sick, and fell asleep. Next morning I woke up there in the willow flats on the cold stones by the river, very weak and cold. My family was worried about me after that. It had been a hot night, so I could say I had stayed out for the cool and had fallen asleep; but my mother knew I was lying about something. She thought it must be that I had come inland with some boy, but for some reason would not admit it. It shamed and worried her to think that I was wearing undyed clothing when I should no longer do so. It enraged me that she should so distrust me, yet I would say nothing to her in denial or explanation. My father knew that I was sick at heart; but it was soon after that that I set the fire, and his worry turned to anger. As for my cousin, she was in love with a Blue Clay boy and interested in nothing else; the girls with whom I gambled had taken to smoking a lot of hemp, which I never liked; and though the friends with whom I rode and looked after the horses were still kind, I did not want to be with humans much, or even with horses. I did not want the world to be as it was. I had begun making up the world.

I made the world this way: that young man of my House in Chukulmas felt as I felt; and I would go to Chukulmas after the Grass, this year. He and I would go up into the hills together and become forest-living people. We would take the roan stallion and go to Looks Up Valley, or farther; we would go to the grass dune country west of the Long Sound, where, he had once told me, the herds of wild horses run. He said that people went from Chukulmas sometimes to catch a wild horse there, but it was country where no human people lived. We would live there together alone, taming and riding the wild horses. Telling myself this world, in the daytime I made us live as brother and sister, but in the nights lying alone I made us make love together. The Grass came and passed; I put off going to Chukulmas, telling myself that it would be better to go after the Sun was danced. I had never danced the Sun as an adult, and I wanted to do that; after that, I told myself, I would go to Chukulmas. All along I knew that if I went or if I did not go it did not matter, and all I wanted was to die.

It is hard to say to yourself that what you want is to die. You keep hiding it behind other things, which you pretend to want. I was impatient for the Twenty-One Days to begin, as if my life would start over with them. On the eve of the first day I went to live at the heyimas.

As soon as I set foot on the ladder my heart went cold and tight. There was a long-singing that night. My lips got numb and my voice would not come out of my throat. I wanted to get out and run away, all night, but I did not know where to go.

Next morning three groups formed: one would go over the northwest range into wild country in silence; one would use hemp and mushrooms for trance; and one would drum and long-sing. I could not choose which group to join, and this distressed me beyond anything. I began shaking, and went to the ladder, but could not lift my foot to climb it.

The old doctor named Gall, who had taught me sometimes at the Doctors Lodge, came down the ladder. She was coming to sing, but the habit of her art distracted her, and she observed me. She turned back and said, "Are you not well?"

"I think I am ill."

"Why is that?"

"I want to dance and can't choose the dancing."

"The long-singing?"

"My voice is gone."

"The trances?"

"I'm afraid of them."

"The journey?"

"I can't leave this house!" I said loudly, and began to shake again.

Gall put her head back with her chin sunk in her neck and looked at me from the tops of her eyes. She was a short, dark, wrinkled woman. She said, "You're already stretched. Do you want to break?"

"Maybe it would be better."

"Maybe it would be better to relax?"

"No, it would be worse."

"There's a choice made. Come now."

Gall took my hand and brought me to the doorway of the inmost room of the heyimas, where the people of the Inner Sun were.

I said, "I can't go in there. I'm not old enough to begin the learning."

Gall said, "Your soul is old." She said the same to Black Oak, who came from the gyre to the doorway: "This is an old soul and a young one, stretching each other too hard."

Black Oak, who was then Speaker of the Serpentine, spoke with Gall, but I was not able to listen to what they said. As soon as we had come into the doorway of the inner room my hair lifted up on my head and my ears sang. I saw round, bright lights coming and going inside the room, where there was no light but the dim shaft from the topmost skylight. The light began to gyre. Black Oak turned to me and spoke, but at that time, as he spoke, the vision began.

I did not see the man Black Oak, but the Serpentine. It was a rock person, not man nor woman, not human, but in shape like a heavy human being, with the blue, bluegreen, and black colors and the surfaces of serpentine rock in its skin. It had no hair, and its eyes were lidless and without transparency, seeing very slowly. Serpentine looked at me very slowly with those rock eyes.

I crouched down in terror. I could not weep or speak or stand or move. I was like a bag full of fear. All I could do was crouch there. I could not breathe at all until a stone, maybe Serpentine's hand, struck my head a hard blow on the right side above the ear. It knocked me off balance and hurt very much, so that I whimpered and sobbed with the pain, and after that I could breathe again. My head did not bleed where it had been struck, but began swelling up there.

I crouched recovering from the blow and the dizziness, and after a long while looked up again. Serpentine was standing there. It stood there. After a while I saw the hands moving slowly. They moved up slowly and came together at the navel, at the middle of the stone. There they pulled back and apart. They pulled open a long, wide rent or opening in the stone, like the doorway of a room, into which I knew I was to enter. I got up crouching and shaking and took a step forward into the stone.

It was not like a room. It was stone, and I was in it. There was no light or breath or room. I think the rest of the vision all took place in the stone; that is where it all happened and was; but because of the human way human people have to see things, it seemed to change, and to be other places, things, and beings.

As if the serpentine rock had crumbled and decayed into the red earth, after a while I was in the earth, part of the dirt. I could feel how the dirt felt. Presently I could feel rain coming into the dirt, coming down. I could feel it in a way that was like seeing, falling down on and into me, out of a sky that was all rain.

I would go to sleep and then be partly awake again, perceiving. I began feeling stones and roots, and along my left side I began to feel and hear cold water running, a creek in the rainy season. Veins of water underground went down and around through me to that creek, seeping in the dark through the dirt and stones. Near the creek I began to feel the big, deep roots of trees, and in the dirt everywhere the fine, many roots of the grasses, the bulbs of brodiea and blue-eyed grass, the ground-squirrel's heart beating, the mole asleep. I began to come up on one of the great roots of a buckeye, up inside the trunk and out the leafless branches to the ends of the small outmost branches. From there I perceived the ladders of rain. These I climbed to the stairways of cloud. These I climbed to the paths of wind. There I stopped, for I was afraid to step out on the wind.

Coyote came down the wind path. She came like a thin woman with rough, dun hair on her head and arms, and a long, fine face with yellow eyes. Two of her children came with her, like coyote pups.

Coyote looked at me and said, "Take it easy. You can look down. You can look back."

I looked back and down under the wind. Below and behind me were dark ridges of forest with the rainbow shining across them, and light shining on the water on the leaves of the trees. I thought there were people on the rainbow, but was not sure of that. Below and farther on were yellow hills of summer and a river among them going to the sea. In places the air below me was so full of birds that I could not see the ground, but only the light on their wings.

Coyote had a high, singing voice like several voices at once. She said, "Do you want to go on from here?"

I said, "I was going to go to the Sun."

"Go ahead. This is all my country." Coyote said that, and then came past me on the wind, trotting on four legs as a coyote, with her pups. I was standing alone on the wind there. So I went on ahead.

My steps on the wind were long and slow, like the Rainbow Dancers' steps. At each step the world below me looked different. At one step it was light, at the next one dark. At the next step it was smoky, at the next clear. At the next long step, black and grey clouds of ash or dust hid everything, and at the next I saw a desert of sand with nothing growing or moving at all. I took a step and everything on the surface of the world was one single town, roofs and ways with people swarming in them like the swarming in pondwater under a lens. I took another step and saw the bottoms of the oceans laid dry, the lava slowly welling from long center seams, and huge desolate canyons far down in the shadow of the walls of the continents, like ditches below the walls of a barn. The next step I took, long and slow on the wind, I saw the surface of the world blank, smooth, and pale, like the face of a baby I once saw that was born without forebrain or eyes. I took one more step and the hawk met me in the sunlight, in the quiet air, over the southwest slope of Grandmother Mountain. It had been raining, and clouds were still dark in the northwest. The rain shone on the leaves of the forests in the canyons of the mountainside.

Of the vision given me in the Ninth House I can tell some parts in writing, and some I can sing with the drum, but for most of it I have not found words or music, though I have spent a good part of my life ever since learning how to look for them. I cannot draw what I saw, as my hand has no gift for making a likeness.

One reason it would be better drawn, and is hard to tell, is that there is no person in it. To tell a story, you say, "I did this," or "She saw that." When there is no I nor she there is no story. I was until I got to the Ninth House; there was the hawk, but I was not. The hawk was; the still air was. Seeing with the hawk's eyes is being without self. Self is mortal. That is the House of Eternity.

So of what the hawk's eyes saw all I can here recall to words is this:

It was the universe of power. It was the network, field, and lines of the energies of all the beings, stars and galaxies of stars, worlds, animals, minds, nerves, dust, the lace and foam of vibration that is being itself, all interconnected, every part part of another part and the whole part of each part, and so comprehensible to itself only as a whole, boundless and unclosed.

At the Exchange it is taught that the electrical mental network of the City extends from all over the surface of the world out past the moon and the other planets to unimaginable distances among the stars: in the vision all that vast web was one momentary glitter of light on one wave on the ocean of the universe of power, one fleck of dust on one grass-seed in unending fields of grass. The images of the light dancing on the waves of the sea or on dustmotes, the glitter of light on ripe grass, the flicker of sparks from a fire, are all I have: no image can contain the vision, which contained all images. Music can mirror it better than words can, but I am no poet to make music of words. Foam, and the scintillation of mica in rock, the flicker and sparkle of waves and dust, the working of the great broadcloth looms, and all dancing, have reflected the hawk's vision for a moment to my mind; and indeed everything would do so, if my mind were clear and strong enough. But no mind or mirror can hold it without breaking.

There was a descent or drawing away, and I saw some things that I can describe. Here is one of them: In this lesser place or plane, which was what might be called the gods or the divine, beings enacted possibilities. These I, being human, recall as having human form. One of them came and shaped the vibrations of energies, closing their paths from gyre into wheel. This one was very strong, and was crippled. He worked as blacksmith at the smithy, making wheels of energy, closed upon themselves, terrible with power, flaming. He who made them was burnt away by them to a shell of cinder, with eyes like a potter's kiln when it is opened, and hair of burning wires, but still he turned the paths of energy and closed them into wheels, locking power into power. All around this being now was black and hollow where the wheels turned and ground and milled. There were other beings who came as if flying, like birds in a storm, flying and crying across the wheels of fire to stop the turning and the work, but they were caught in the wheels, and burst like feathers of flame. The miller was a thin shell of darkness now, very weak, burnt out, and he too was caught in the wheels' turning and burning and grinding, and was ground to dust, like fine black meal. The wheels as they turned kept growing and joining until the whole machine was interlocked cog within cog, and strained, and brightened, and burst into pieces. Every wheel as it burst was a flare of faces and eyes and flowers and beasts on fire, burning, exploding, destroyed, falling into black dust. That happened, and it was one flicker of brightness and dark in the universe of power, a bubble of foam, a flick of the shuttle, a fleck of mica. The dark dust or meal lay in the shape of open curves or spirals. It began to move and shift, and there was a scintillation in it, like dust in a shaft of sunlight. It began dancing. Then the dancing drew away and drew away, and closer by, to the left, something was there crying like a little animal. That was myself, my mind and being in the world; and I began to become myself again; but my soul that had seen the vision was not entirely willing. Only my mind kept drawing it back to me from the Ninth House, calling and crying for it till it came.

I was lying on my right side on earth, in a small, warm room with earthen walls. The only light came from the red bar of an electric heater. Somewhere nearby people were singing a two-note chant. I was holding in my left hand a rock of serpentine, greenish with dark markings, quite round as if waterworn, though serpentine does not often wear round but splits and crumbles. It was just large enough that I could close my fingers around it. I held this round stone for a long time and listened to the chanting, until I went to sleep. When I woke up, after a while I felt the rock going immaterial, so that my fingers began sinking into it, and it weighed less and less, until it was gone. I was a little grieved by this, for I had thought it a remarkable thing to come back from the Right Arm of the World with a piece of it in my hand; but as I grew clearer-headed I perceived the vanity of that notion. Years later the rock came back to me. I was walking down by Moon Creek with my sons when they were small boys. The younger one saw the rock in the water and picked it up, saying, "A world!" I told him to keep it in his heya-box, which he did. When he died, I put that rock back in the water of Moon Creek.

I had been in the vision for the first two days and nights of the Twenty-One Days of the Sun. I was very weak and tired, and they kept me in the heyimas all the rest of the Twenty-One Days. I could hear the long-singing, and sometimes I went into other rooms of the heyimas; they made me welcome even in the inmost room, where they were singing and dancing the Inner Sun, and where I had entered the vision. I would sit and listen and half-watch. But if I tried to follow the dancing with my eyes, or sing, or even touch the tongue-drum, the weakness would wash into me like a wave on sand, and I would go back into the little room and lie down on the earth, in the earth.

They waked me to listen to the Morning Carol; that was the first time in twenty-one days that I climbed the ladder and saw the sun, that day, the day of the Sun Rising.

The people dancing the Inner Sun had been in charge of

me. They had told me that I was in danger, and that if I approached another vision I should try to turn away from it, as I was not strong enough for it yet. They had told me not to dance; and they kept bringing me food, so good and so kindly given that I could not refuse it, and ate it with enjoyment. After the Sun Risen days were past, certain scholars of the heyimas took me in their charge. Tarweed, a man of my House, and the woman Milk of the Obsidian, were my guides. It was now time that I begin to learn the recounting of the vision.

When I began, I thought there was nothing to learn: all I had to do was say what I had seen.

Milk worked with words; Tarweed worked with words, drum, and matrix chanting. They had me go very slowly, telling very little at a time, sometimes one word only, and repeating what I had been able to tell, singing it with the matrix chant, so that as much as possible might be truly recalled and given, and could be recalled and given again.

When I began thus to find out what it is to say what one has seen, and when the great complexity and innumerable vivid details of the vision overwhelmed my imagination and surpassed my ability to describe, I feared that I would lose it all before I could grasp one fragment of it, and that even if I remembered some of it I would never understand any of it. My guides reassured me and quieted my impatience. Milk said, "We have some training in this craft, and you have none. You have to learn to speak sky with an earth tongue. Listen: if a baby were carried up the Mountain, could she walk back down, until she learned to walk?"

Tarweed explained to me that as I learned to apprehend mentally what I had perceived in vision, I would approach the condition of living in both Towns; and so, he said, "there's no great hurry."

I said, "But it will take years and years!"

He said, "You've been at it for a thousand years already. Gall said you were an old soul."

It bothered me that I was often not sure whether Tarweed was joking or not joking. That always bothers young people, and however old my soul might be, my mind was fifteen. I had to live a while before I understood that a lot of things can be said joking and not joking at the same time. I had to come clear back to Coyote's House from the Hawk's House to learn that, and sometimes I still forget it.

Tarweed's way was joking, shocking, stirring, but he was gentle; I had no fear of him. I had been afraid of Milk ever since she had looked at me in the Blood Lodge and said, "What are you here for?" She was a great scholar and was Singer of the Lodge. Her way was calm, patient, impersonal, but she was not gentle, and I feared her. With Tarweed she was polite, but it was plain that her manners masked contempt. She thought a man's place was in the woods and fields and workshops, not among sacred and intellectual things. In the Lodge I had heard her say the old gibe, "A man fucks with his brain and thinks with his penis." Tarweed knew well enough what she thought, but intellectual men are used to having their capacities doubted and their achievements snubbed; he did not seem to mind her arrogance as much as I sometimes did, even to the point of trying to defend him against her once, saying, "Even if he is a man he thinks like a woman!"

It did no good, of course; and if it was partly true, it wasn't wholly true, because the thing that was most important of all to me I could not speak of to Tarweed, a man, and a man of my House; and to Milk, arrogant and stern as she was, and a woman who had lived all her life celibate, I did not even need to speak of it. I began to, once, feeling that I must, and she stopped me. "What is proper for me to know of this, I know," she said. "Vision is transgression! The vision is to be shared; the transgression cannot be."

I did not understand that. I was very much afraid of going out of the heyimas and being caught in my old life again, going the wrong way again in false thinking and despair. A half-month or so after the Sun, I began to feel and say that I was still weak and ill, and could not leave the heyimas. To this Tarweed said, "Aha! About time for you to go home!"

I thought him most unfeeling. When I was working with Milk, in my worry I began crying, and presently I said, "I wish I had never had this vision!"

Milk looked at me, a glance across the eyes, like being whipped in the face with a thin branch. She said, "You did not have a vision."

I snivelled and stared at her.

"You had nothing. You have nothing. The house stands. You can live in a corner of it, or all of it, or go outside it, as you choose." So Milk said, and left me.

I stayed alone in the small room. I began to look at it, the small warm room with earth walls and floor and roof, underground. The walls were earth: the whole earth. Outside them was the sky: the whole sky. The room was the universe of power. I was in my vision. It was not in me.

So I went home to live and try to stay on the right way.

Part of most days I went to the heyimas to study with Tarweed or to the Blood Lodge to study with Milk. My health was sound, but I was still tired and sleepy, and my household did not get very much work out of me. All my family but my father were busy, restless people, eager to work and talk but never to be still. Among them, after the month in the heyimas, I felt like a pebble in a mountain creek, bounced and buffeted. But I could go to work with my father. Milk had suggested to him that he take me with him when he worked. Tarweed had questioned her about that, saying that the craft was spiritually dangerous, and Milk had replied, in the patient, patronizing tone she used to men, "Don't worry about that. It was danger that enabled her."

So I went back to working with power. I learned the art carefully and soberly, and set no more fires. I learned drumming with Tarweed, and speaking mystery with Milk. But it was all slow, slow, and my fear kept growing: fear and impatience. The image of the roan horse's rider was not in my mind, as it had been, but was the center of my fear. I never went to ride, and kept away from my friends who cared for the horses, and stayed out of the pastures where the horses were. I tried never to think about the Summer dancing, the games and races. I tried never to think about lovemaking, although my mother's sister had a new husband and they made love every night in the next room with a good deal of noise. I began to fear and dislike myself, and fasted and purged to weaken myself.

I told Tarweed nothing of all this, shame preventing me; nor did I ever speak of it to Milk, fear preventing me.

So the World was danced, and next would come the Moon. The thought of that dance made me more and more frightened; I felt trapped by it. When the first night of the Moon came I went down into my heyimas, meaning to stay there the whole time, closing my ears to the lovesongs. I started drumming a vision-tune that Tarweed had brought back from his dragonfly visions. Almost at once I entered trance, and went into the house of anger.

In that house it was black and hot, with a yellowish glimmering like heat lightning, and a dull muttering noise underfoot and in the walls. There was an old woman in there, very black, with too many arms. She called me, not by the name I then had, Berry, but Flicker: "Flicker, come here! Flicker, come here!" I understood that Flicker was my name, but I did not come.

The old woman said, "What are you sulking about? Why don't you go fuck with your brother in Chukulmas? Desire unacted is corruption. Must Not is a slave-owner, Ought Not is a slave. Energy constrained turns the wheels of evil. Look what you're dragging with you! How can you run the gyre, how can you handle power, chained like that? Superstition! Superstition!"

I found that my legs were both fastened with bolts and

hasps to a huge boulder of serpentine rock, so that I could not move at all. I thought that if I fell down, the boulder would roll on me and crush me.

The old woman said, "What are you wearing on your head? That's no Moon Dance veil. Superstition! Superstition!"

I put up my hands and found my head covered with a heavy helmet made of black obsidian. I was seeing and hearing through this black, murky glass, which came down over my eyes and ears.

"Take it off, Flicker!" the old woman said.

I said, "Not at your bidding!"

I could hardly see or hear her, as the helmet pressed heavier and thicker on my head, and the boulder pushed against my legs and back.

She cried, "Break free! You are turning into stone! Break free!"

I would not obey her. I chose to disobey. With my hands I pressed the obsidian helmet into my ears and eyes and forehead until it sank in and became part of me, and I pushed myself back into the boulder until it became part of my legs and body. Then I stood there, very stiff and heavy and hard, but I could walk, and I could see and hear, now that the dark glass was not over my ears and eyes but was part of them. I saw that the house was all on fire, burning and smouldering, floor, walls, and roof. A black bird, a crow, was flying in the smoke from one room to the next. The old woman was burning, her clothes and flesh and hair smouldering. The crow flew around her and cried to me, "Sister, get out, you'd better get out!"

There is nothing but anger in the house of anger. I said, "No!"

The crow cawed, saying, "Sister, fetch water, water of the spring!" Then it flew out through the burning wall of the house. Just as it went it looked back at me with a man's face, beautiful and strong, with curly fiery hair streaming upward. Then the walls of fire sank down into the walls of the Serpentine heyimas where I was sitting drumming on the three-note drum. I was still drumming, but a different pattern, a new one.

After that vision I was called Flicker; the scholars agreed that it's best to use the name that that Grandmother gives you, even if you don't do what she says. After that vision I went up to the Springs of the River, as Crow had said to do; and after it I was freed from my fear of my desire.

The central vision is central, it is not for anything outside itself; indeed there is nothing outside it. What I beheld in the Ninth House is, as a cloud or a mountain is. We make use of such visions, make meanings out of them, find images in them, live on them, but they are not for us or about us, any more than the world is. We are part of them. There are other kinds of vision, all farther from the center and nearer to the mortal self; one of those is the turning vision, which is about a person's own life. The vision in which that Grandmother named me was a turning vision.

The Summer came, and the people came down from Chukulmas. My brother of the Serpentine did not ride his roan horse in the races; a girl of the Obsidian of Chukulmas rode that horse, and he rode a sorrel mare. The roan stallion won all races, and was much praised. After that summer he would race no more, but be put to stud, they said. I did not ride, but watched the races and the games. It is hard to say how I felt. My throat ached all the time, and I kept saying silently inside myself, goodbye, goodbye! But what I was saying goodbye to was already gone. I was mourning and yet unmoved. The girl was a good rider, and beautiful, and I thought, maybe they are going to come inland together; but it did not hurt or concern me. What I wanted was to be gone from Telina, to begin living the life that followed the turning vision, that followed the gyre.

So in the heat of the summertime I went with Tarweed upriver, to the Springs of the River at Wakwaha.

On the Mountain I lived in the host-house of the Serpentine, and worked mostly as electrician's assistant at odd jobs around the sacred buildings and the Archive and Exchange.

In the morning I would come outdoors at sunrise. All beyond and below the porch of that house I would see a vast pluming blankness, the summer fog filling the Valley, while the first rays of the sun brightened the rocks of the Mountain's peaks above me, and I would sing as I had been taught:

> It is the Valley of the puma,
> where the lion walks,
> where the lion wakes,
> shining, shining in the Seventh House!

Later, in the rainy season, the puma walked on the Mountain itself, darkening the summits and the Springs in cloud and grey mist. To wake in the silence of that rainless, all-concealing fog was to wake to dream, to breathe the lion's breath.

Much of each day on the Mountain I spent in the heyimas, and at times slept there. I worked with the scholars and visionaries of Wakwaha at the techniques of revisioning, of recounting, and of music. I did not practice dancing or painting much, as I had no gift for them, but practiced recalling and recounting in spoken and written language and with the drum.

I had, as many people have, exaggerated notions of how visionaries live. I expected a strained, athletic, ascetic existence, always stretched towards the ineffable. In fact, it was a dull kind of life. When people are in vision they can't look after themselves, and when they come back from it they may be extremely tired, or excited and bewildered, and in either case need quietness without distractions and demands. In other words, it's like childbearing, or any hard, intense work. One supports and protects the worker. Revisioning and recounting are much the same, though not quite so hard.

In the host-house I fasted only before the great wakwa; I ate lightly, with some care of which foods I ate, and drank little wine, and watered it. If you are going into vision or revision you don't want to keep changing yourself and going in a different way—through starving one time, the next time through drunkenness, or cannabis, or trance-singing, or whatever. What you want is moderation and continuity. If one is an ecstatic, of course it's another matter; that is not work, but burning.

So the life I led in Wakwaha was dull and peaceful, much the same from day to day and season to season, and suited and pleased my mind and heart so that I desired nothing else. All the work I did, in those years on the Mountain, was revisioning and recounting the vision of the Ninth House that had been given me; I gave all I could of it to the scholars of the Serpentine for their records and interpretations, in which our guidance as a people lies. They were kind, true kin, family of my House, and I at last a child of that House again, not self-exiled. I thought I had come home, and would live there all my life, telling and drumming, going into vision and coming back from it, dancing in the beautiful dancing place of the Five High Houses, drinking from the Springs of the River.

The Grass was late, in the third year I lived in Wakwaha. Some days after it ended and some days before the Twenty-One Days began, I was about to go up the ladder of the Serpentine heyimas when Hawk Woman came to me. I thought she was one of the people of the heyimas, until she cried the hawk's cry, "kiyir, kiyir!" I turned, and she said, "Dance the Sun upon the Mountain, Flicker, and after that go down. Maybe you should learn how to dye cloth." She laughed, and flew up as the hawk through the entrance overhead.

Other people came where I was standing at the foot of the ladder. They had heard the hawk's cry, and some saw her fly up through the entrance of the heyimas.

After that I had neither vision nor revision of the Ninth House or any house or kind.

I was bereft, and relieved. That terrible grandeur had been hard to bear, to bring back, to share and give and lose over and over. It had all been beyond my strength, and I was not sorry to cease revisioning. But when I thought that I had lost all vision, and must soon leave Wakwaha, I began to grieve. I thought about those people whom I had thought were my kinfolk, long ago when I was a child, before I was afraid. They were gone, and now I too must go, leaving these kinfolk of my House of Wakwaha, and go live among strangers the rest of my life.

A woman-living man of the Serpentine of Wakwaha, Deertongue, who had taught me and sung with me and given me friendship, saw that I was downcast and anxious, and said to me, "Listen. You think everything is done. Nothing is done. You think the door is shut. No door is shut. What did Coyote say to you, at the beginning of it all?"

I said, "She said to take it easy."

Deertongue nodded his head and laughed.

I said, "But Hawk said to go down."

"She didn't say not to come back."

"But I have lost the visions!"

"But you have your wits! Where is the center of your life, Flicker?"

I thought not very long, and answered, "There. In that vision. In the Ninth House."

He said, "Your life turns on that center. Only don't blind your intellect by hankering after vision! You know that the vision is not your self. The hawk turns upon the hawk's desire. You will come round home and find the door wide open."

I danced the Sun upon the Mountain, as Hawk Woman had said to do, and after that I began to feel that I must go. There were some people living in Wakwaha who sought vision or ecstasy by continuous fasting or drug-taking, and lived in hallucination; such people came not to know vision from imagination, and lived without honesty, making up the world all the time. I was afraid that if I stayed there I might begin imitating them, as Deertongue had warned me. After all, I had gone wrong that way once before. So I said goodbye to people, and on a cold bright morning I went down the Mountain. A young redwing hawk circled crying over the canyons, "kiyir! kiyir!"—so mournfully that I cried myself.

I went back to my mothers' household in Telina-na. My uncle had married and moved out, so I had his small room to myself; that was a good thing, since my cousin had married and had a child and the household was as crowded and restless as ever. I went back to work with my father, learning both theory and practice with him, and after two years I became a member of the Millers Art. He and I continued to work together often. My life was nearly as quiet as it had been in Wakwaha. Sometimes I would spend days in the heyimas drumming; there were no visions, but the silence inside the drumming was what I wanted.

So the seasons went along, and I was thinking about what Hawk Woman had said. I was rewiring an old house, Seven Steps House in the northeast arm of Telina, and while I was working there on a hot day a man of one of the households brought me some lemonade, and we fell to talking, and so again the next day. He was a Blue Clay man from Chukulmas who had married a Serpentine woman of Telina. They had been given two children, the younger born sevai. She had left the children with him and left her mothers' house, going across town to marry a Red Adobe man. I knew her;, she was one of the people I had gambled with as a child, but I had never talked to this man, Stillwater, who lived in his children's grandmother's house. He worked mostly as a chemist and tanner and housekeeper. We talked, and got on well, and met to talk again. I came inland with him, and we decided to marry.

My father was against it, because Stillwater had two children in his household already and so I would bear none; but that was what I wanted. My grandmother and mother were not heartily for anything I did, because I had always disappointed them, and they did not want three more people in our house, which was crowded enough. But that, too, was what I wanted. Everything I wanted in those years came to be.

Stillwater and the little boys and I made a household on the ground floor of Seven Steps House, where their grandmother lived on the first floor. She was a lazy, sweet-tempered woman, very fond of Stillwater and the children, and we got on very well. We lived in that house fourteen years. All that time I had what I wanted, and was contented, like a ewe with two lambs in a safe pasture, with my head down eating the grass. All that time was like a long day in summer, in the fenced fields, or in a quiet house when the doors are closed to keep the rooms cool. That was my life's day. Before it and after it were the twilights and the dark, when things and the shadows of things become one.

Our elder son—and this was a satisfaction to my grandmother at last—went to learn with the Doctors Lodge on White Sulphur Creek as soon as he entered his sprouting years, and by the time he was twenty he was living at the Lodge much of the time. The younger died when he had lived sixteen years. Living with his pain and always increasing weakness and seeing him lose the use of his hands and the sight in his eyes had driven his brother to seek to be a healer, but living with his fearless soul had been my chief joy. He was like a little hawk that came into one's hands for the warmth, for a moment, fearless and harmless, but hurt. After he died, Stillwater lost heart, and began longing for his old home. Presently he went back to Chukulmas to live in his mother's house. Sometimes I went to visit him there.

I went back to my childhood home, my mothers' house, where my grandmother and mother and father and aunt and cousin and her husband and two children were. They were still busy and noisy; it was not where I wanted to be. I would go to the heyimas and drum, but that was not what I wanted, either. I missed Stillwater's company, but it was no longer the time for us to live together; that was done. It was something else I wanted, but I could not find out what.

In the Blood Lodge one day they told me that Milk, who was now truly an old woman, had had a stroke. My son came with me to see her, and helped her in her recovery; and since she was alone, I went to stay with her while she needed help. It suited her to have me there, and so I lived with her. It was comfortable for both of us; but she was looking for her last name and learning how to die, and although I could be of some help to her while she did that, and could learn from her, it wasn't what I wanted myself, yet.

One day a little before the Summer I was working in the

storage barns above Moon Creek. The Art had put in a new generator there, and I was checking out the wiring to the threshers, some of which needed reinsulation; the mice had been at it. I was working away there in a dark, dusty crawl-space, hearing the mice scuttering about overhead in the rafters and between the walls. Presently I noticed with part of my attention that several people were in the crawl-space with me, watching what I was doing. They were greyish-brown people with long, slender, white hands and feet, and bright eyes; I had never seen them before, but they seemed familiar. I said, while I went on working, "I wish you would not take the insulation off the wires. A fire could start. There must be better things to eat in a grain barn!"

The people laughed a little, and the darkest one said in a high, soft voice, "Bedding."

They looked behind them then, and went away quickly and quietly. Somebody else was there. I felt one little chill of fear. At first I couldn't see him clearly in that twilight of the crawl-space; then I saw it was Tarweed.

"You never ride horses any more, Flicker," he said.

"Riding is for the young, Tarweed," I said.

"Are you old?"

"Nearly forty years old."

"And you don't miss riding?"

He was teasing me, as people had teased me once about being in love with the roan horse.

"No, I don't miss that."

"What do you miss?"

"My child that died."

"Why should you miss him?"

"He is dead."

"So am I," said Tarweed. And so he was. He had died five years ago.

So I knew then what it was I missed, what I wanted. It was only not to be shut into the House of Earth. I did not have to go in and out the doors, if only I could see those who did. There was Tarweed, and he laughed a little, like the mice.

He did not say anything more, but watched me in the shadows. When I was done with the work, he was gone. When I left the barn, I saw the barn owl high up on a rafter, sleeping.

I went home to Milk's household. I told her at supper about Tarweed and the mice.

She listened, and began to cry a little. She was weak, since the stroke, and her fierceness sometimes turned to tears. She said, "You were always ahead of me, going ahead of me!"

I had never known that she envied me. It made me sad to know it, and yet I wanted to laugh at the way we waste our feelings. "Somebody has to open the door!" I said. I showed her the people who were coming into the room, the kind of people I used to see when I was a young child. I knew they were indeed my kin, but I did not know who they were. I asked Milk, "Who are they?"

She was bewildered at first, and could not see well, and complained. The people began to speak, and she to answer. Sometimes they spoke this language, and sometimes I did not understand what they said; but she answered them eagerly.

When she grew tired, they went away quietly, and I helped her to bed. As she began to sleep, I saw a little child come and lie down beside her. She put her arms around it. Every night after that until Milk died in the winter, the child came to her bed to sleep.

Once I spoke of it, saying, "your daughter." Milk looked at me with that whipping look in her one good eye. She said, "Not my daughter. Yours."

So I keep that house now, with the daughter I never bore, the child of my first love, and with others of my family. Sometimes when I sweep the floor of that house I see the dust in a shaft of sunlight, dancing in curves and spirals, flickering.

Notes to *The Visionary*

p. 4: *vetulou* — A game resembling polo, but played with an openwork wicker ball, scooped and thrown by long-handled wicker scoops.

p. 5: *sevai* — Sevai means sheathed. It was a congenital degenerative condition, related to residual ancient toxins in soil and water, affecting the motor nerves and eventually the sympathetic nervous system. In some regions of the planet it was not very common, in others it was; in the Valley as many as one in four conceptions was stillborn due to sevai. As Flicker says, the later the condition declared itself the slower and milder its progress usually was, but always tending inexorably toward incapacity, paralysis, and death.

p. 17: *scholar* — Ayanda means both teacher and student, learned and learner, as does our word scholar. The scholars of a heyimas were women and men with a strong religious or intellectual bent; they kept that House.

p. 19: *living in both Towns* — An unusual image for the two Arms of the World; the nine Houses of Earth and of Sky.

p. 22: *Flicker* — Shoko means both the big woodpecker called flicker in California, and a dipping, jumping, dancing recurrent movement.

This first volume of the
Capra Back-to-Back Series
was printed for Capra Press
by Kingsport Press in Kingsport, Tennesee.
Two hundred copies were
numbered and signed by the author.

———————

Illustrations and cover portraits
by Margaret Chodos.

Typography and design by Jim Cook
for Cook/Sundstrom Associates.

This first volume of the
Capra Back-to-Back Series
was printed for Capra Press
by Kingsport Press in Kingsport, Tennesee.
Two hundred copies were
numbered and signed by the author.

Illustrations and cover portraits
by Margaret Chodos.

Typography and design by Jim Cook
for Cook/Sundstrom Associates.

Jean hugged him about the frail ribs and hurriedly kissed him on each gray-bearded cheek. By the time Jean boarded the ship and turned to look back from the stern, Papa was gone.

When the ship swung out into the river's current, Jean was still leaning against the rail. The spires and slate roofs and pigeon-filled sky of Nantes slipped away behind. The riverbank, familiar as his own face in the mirror, slipped away. Everything was slipping away, and he was adrift, exiled, alone, bound for another strange country. Passing Coueron, he eagerly scanned the quay, and there the four women stood, Cook flapping her apron, Elizabeth and *Maman* fluttering their handkerchiefs, Rosa waving her straw hat with its pink streamers. Memories of other departures seized him. With a show of courage he lifted his arm and waved it bravely for them to see, for all of France to see. When he could no longer make out their dwindling figures on the quay, he turned sharply around and walked on quick steps toward the bow, his soul in turmoil, his face set hard to the west.

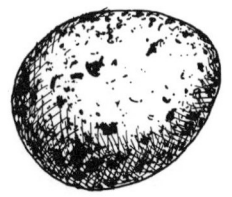

"Go!" said Papa, and the wagon jerked into motion.

Jean was in such a tumult of eagerness to be gone and regret at leaving that he rolled along the familiar road into Nantes without seeing the river, the meadows, the hunched cottages, without hearing Papa's chatter. He opened the first volume of Buffon across his lap and blindly stroked the marbled endpapers. He thumbed the pages idly, pausing at the hook-beaked vulture, the haughty eagle, the goshawk tearing apart a rabbit, the bloody buzzard, but he could not pay attention to the words. He rolled along oblivious, rapt. All that broke through his inner turbulence was a pang of fear about getting caught, bound, and delivered into Napoleon's army.

At the foot of the gangplank they were met by Captain Smith and a sourfaced customs official whom Jean recognized as a cardplaying crony of Papa's. The three men exchanged jokes in a mixture of French and English while Jean, gripping the passport in sweaty palms, waited anxiously in Papa's shadow.

After the pleasantries, the customs official took the passport and examined it scrupulously.

Jean held his breath. Let me go, he thought in a fury. Let me go, or I will fling you aside and rush on board and throttle anyone who comes after me.

At length the official returned the passport and announced in a boisterous tone, "May you enjoy the visit to your native Louisiana, Monsieur Audubon! May you spend more time wrestling with the Creole girls than with the crocodiles!"

All three men laughed at this and thumped one another on the back. Papa started coughing, and he was still coughing when

"They're the first three volumes on the birds," said Rosa. "They have much the loveliest illustrations."

"Is it what you wanted?" *Maman* asked eagerly.

Jean was speechless with delight. He flung his arms about each of them in turn, first *Maman*, who leaned heavily against him like a piece of earth, then womanly Rosa, plump Cook, dear Elizabeth, still bone-crushingly powerful even though her midnight skin was wrinkled and her hair was white, and last of all Papa, fierce Papa, tyrant Papa, who felt smaller and frailer than any of the women.

The sound of a man's shout rose from the street.

"The wagon!" said Rosa.

"So soon?" *Maman* wailed, as if in pain. "How can it be?"

There was a hasty shutting of trunks, buckling of straps, tying of bundles. Two burly teamsters in leather aprons clumped up the stairs and wrestled baggage onto their shoulders and clumped back down again, upstairs and down, five trips, before they had the wagon loaded. Still clutching the volumes of Buffon, Jean distributed kisses and hasty, unthinking promises. Yes, he would write letters. He would keep his feet dry. He would take care about his food, shun the head-spinning spiritous liquors, and keep his distance from the ladies, those wily American ladies.

Goodbye, goodbye, goodbye. The wagondriver gave a shrill whistle. Tugging free of their arms, Jean backed into the street. The women stopped at the front gate, their handkerchiefs lifted, their faces awry with grief, while Jean and Papa climbed into the wagon.

"I said you won't even dream of marriage before you come back home," *Maman* repeated anxiously.

"He will learn English and attend to business, is what he will do," declared Papa.

Before Jean could stammer a reply, Rosa thrust her parcel into his arms and said, "This is for you."

Looking at her over the brown package, Jean realized with a sharp pang of longing how much he would miss her, his whimpering, wheedling, tattling sister, who had grown suddenly into a young lady, a target for the hungers of men. One moment she had seemed little more than a bundle in a blanket, and the next moment here she was wrapped in a woman's flesh. Stupidly clutching the heavy parcel, he blinked at her, then at each of them in turn, Papa and *Maman*, Elizabeth and Cook, feeling the sudden ache of their absence. He would sail to America, and their lives would go on here, without him.

They all gathered around him and gazed expectantly. *Maman* and Elizabeth even broke into bittersweet smiles of anticipation.

"Well, aren't you going to open it?" said Rosa.

"Of course, of course." Jean set the weight down on a trunk and fumbled at the knots. The circle of expectant faces drew close about him. He stripped away the paper, disclosing three fat leatherbound books. With hands shaking, he tipped the first volume so as to read the spine, where the crown and fleur-de-lis of headless King Louis were stamped in gold. Could it be? Yes! "Buffon!" he cried joyfully, "My own copies of Buffon! Let me see which ones," and hastily searched for the title page.

not mix in the politics of that volatile country. Keep away from the wilderness territory, where business is poor and the savages are bloodthirsty. Beware of the women, who are very free in America, especially the English."

"As free as cats in the alley," *Maman* put in. "Your papa knows whereof he speaks."

Papa cleared his throat, giving her a look that had a bit of the old fire in it. "Many of them wander about entirely without chaperons. The poorest girls mix indiscriminately with the richest, and the ones with the least money also display the fewest scruples. They will show you their tiny feet and expect you to marry them, however empty their purse might be."

Women rose and set like rosy moons in Jean's thoughts as he trooped restlessly from wall to wall of his room. With an effort he banished them, and thought of America. A blank slate. Would the hour of sailing never come? He ached to be gone, free, away from the entanglements of *Maman*'s superstitions and Papa's ambitions and the sullying memories of boyhood.

"I'm sure he has no thought of marriage," said *Maman*. "Isn't that so, sweetheart?" Receiving no answer, she called plaintively, "Jean?"

"Pardon?" He stopped short. Rosa, following at his heels, bumped into him and nearly tripped under the weight of the bulky parcel she was carrying. Grabbing her waist to keep her from falling, Jean was amazed at the softness of his little sister. When had she filled out so? He could remember when she used to feel as stiff as a wooden doll.

priest, except for your godless carrying on—my son is to mix with Quakers! Why not snake-worshippers? Hah? Why not sword-swallowers? Why not cannibals?"

"Calm yourself, Mother, calm yourself," Papa soothed.

Maman persevered: "You will be a good Catholic, my Jean, won't you? You will remember your catechism, and no matter what foolishness other people practice, you will hold to the true Church?"

"Yes," Jean replied dutifully, wanting to silence the old quarrel, "yes, dear *Maman*," even though he remembered little more from his catechism than the smell of the calfbound volume of Bossuet, the priest's bad teeth, and a few phrases: *Born of the Father before all ages. God of God, light of light, true God of true God. The water of wisdom and dew of divine inspiration. The Father incomprehensible, the Son incomprehensible, and the Holy Ghost incomprehensible.* All of it, in truth, was incomprehensible to him, the mysteries of heaven and hell and purgatory, as well as the mysteries of his *maman*'s passionate faith and his papa's passionate disbelief.

Maman knotted the stockings into a ball in her fist. "And if this venture in business fails," she pleaded, "you will come home to me and study for the priesthood, is that not so?"

Papa let out a scoffing burst of breath.

"Yes, yes," said Jean, "whatever you like, *Maman*." Odor of incense, furtive motions of the priest at the altar. Cathedrals locked, and then, at Napoleon's order, cathedrals flung open again. Did God play hide and seek?

While Jean paced, Papa resumed his parting homily: "Do

the outermost settlement, all the way north to the Pole and west to the Pacific, stretched the wilderness, the bear-haunted, wolf-haunted, bird-haunted wilderness!

On the day his ship was to sail, while the womenfolk stowed the last few items in his trunk and Papa delivered a monologue of parting instructions, Jean was feverish with excitement. Unable to sit down, he paced about the bedroom, occasionally halting at the window to look outside for the wagon that would deliver him to the quay at Nantes. Folding shirts, *Maman* and Elizabeth were weeping openly, but he scarcely noticed. Cook bustled in with apples, sugar water, freshly-baked bread, as if she doubted there would be any food on the ship. Rosa followed him around the bedroom like a puppy, her arms filled with clothes, saying little but never letting him out of her sight.

"Do not accept paper money," Papa was advising in a harsh crow's voice. "Always demand coin or a letter of credit. Never do business after drinking or on a full stomach. Sleep with your wallet under the pillow whenever you travel. Observe the religious practices of your neighborhood."

Maman interrupted her weeping to exclaim, "He will attend Catholic mass and nothing else!"

"Not if he finds himself surrounded by Quakers or Methodists," Papa declared irritably.

"Quakers and Methodists!" *Maman* stopped packing the trunk, holding suspended from her hand a pair of gray cotton stockings like limp fish. "My son, who might have become a arrived. And soon after that an old comrade of Papa's from the American revolution, Captain John Smith of New England, agreed to give Jean secret passage aboard his ship. "Why must every name be written down on the passenger list, eh?" Captain Smith declared jovially while drinking brandy with Papa and Jean in the garden beside the fishpond.

"Why indeed!" said Papa in his best prison English. "Simply because Napoleon wishes to conquer the world, is that any reason for me to make him a gift of my only son?"

"And do you fancy yourself a future in America, lad?" said Captain Smith.

"It is a celebrated country," Jean answered, trying not to show his intense excitement.

Since that day when his passage had been arranged, Jean had thought of little else besides America. Land of romance and new beginnings! No one there would know of his flight from Napoleon's army, or his failures, or his bastard birth. Judging by what he had read of that vast continent in the nouvelles of Chateaubriand and the letters of de Crevecoeur, and by what he had heard Papa and other travelers say, America was an almost magical place where anything might come to pass. Overnight wealth, sojourns among savage tribes, unlimited free land awaiting discovery. On the mighty Mississippi River—beside which the Loire would seem like a puny creek—flamingos coasted along on rafts of flowers. Snakes curled themselves into hoops and went rolling across the prairies. There were waterfalls higher than the grandest mountain in France. And beyond earshot. John remembered having quaked as a child whenever Papa had so much as raised an eyebrow. But now the retired captain walked with a stoop, appeared at midday in his embroidered Chinese dressing gown, coughed wretchedly for much of the night, and spoke often in a beseeching, uncertain voice. He moaned from the aching of his old wounds. He complained aloud that his pension was niggardly. Never had he been promoted to the rank he deserved. He would not realize a centime from his vast holdings in Saint-Domingue, not a centime. And as for France, grand France, she was going to rack and ruin, and that tyrant Napoleon was betraying the Revolution.

Despite these other complaints, Jean could not help believing that his own failure at the academy, at school—indeed at almost every task Papa had set for him—was the real cause of Papa's decline. The old man rarely spoke of those disappointments. In truth, until Jean turned eighteen and Napoleon's recruiters began calling at the house, Papa had all but given up speaking to him. Night after night Jean would fish for his approval, showing him some new sketches, playing a new melody on the flute, telling of a riotous caper with chums from Nantes; yet Papa would merely swing a dim gaze in his direction and mutter a few broken sentences.

But when the recruiters knocked at the door of the villa and demanded to see Jean's birth certificate, Papa blazed up with renewed life. Immediately he began contacting his old republican friends who still held a few strings of power. Within a day the recruiters were called off. A week later the false passport how? I am hungry. This food that we eat, it is called what?" As he spoke, Yvette concentrated on his lips and her eyes grew round again in admiration.

This speech nearly exhausted his knowledge of the language, even though for weeks Papa had been shuffling after him through the house and garden on slippered feet, wheezing English. "Jean," Papa would call, and then correct himself, "*John*, will you stop and listen to me? Observe my mouth when I tell you the words. *Dinner engagement. Banknote. Thank you for your kindness. The barn is full of grain. Charmed, I am sure, my dear lady.*"

Six years it took Papa to learn all these words in English prisons, Jean thought, and he expects me to learn the same in six days! "Surely," he objected, "they are not so backward as to be ignorant of French."

But Papa insisted: "They are, they are! Perfectly ignorant!"

"Don't worry, I shall master the language quickly enough once I am living among them," Jean proclaimed, but finally he was compelled to leave the house in order to escape Papa's English lessons.

These days Papa rarely went outdoors, unless it was to putter around in the barnyard clucking at geese or patting the fluffy sheep or peering at silvery shapes in the fishpond. The keeping of animals seemed to Jean a curious pastime for an old salt. It troubled him, on the eve of his departure, to see how sadly Papa had withered. Until his retirement from the navy two years ago, the old man had been a commanding presence, upright in bearing, fierce of tongue, a terror to everyone within its effect upon the ladies. "But how else am I to restore the family fortunes?"

"Can you truly manage among those shrewd Yankees and wild Indians? Are you not afraid of crossing savannahs filled with buffalo and rivers crowded with crocodiles?"

Drawing his eyebrows together, he fixed the vague, hair-framed face with a worldly stare. "Do not be afraid for me. All my life I have been preparing for this opportunity. And I shall seize it!" He raised a fist in demonstration. "Wait for me, precious," he told her, as he had told half a dozen other girls. "In a year, or perhaps two, I shall return as a wealthy merchant, accompanied by a fleet of my own ships."

"And you are certain the recruiters will permit you to leave France?" Yvette asked delicately.

"Certain." Leaning so close that he could see the tiny pale hairs in the convolutions of her ear, Jean whispered, "The First Consul himself has given the order."

"Bonaparte!" Yvette cried, raising a gloved hand to her lips.

"Yes," Jean whispered. "You see, I am to manage a lead mine on my father's estate in Pennsylvania, and Napoleon depends on me to ship back everything I produce for the armies of France."

Still holding the gloved fingers to her lips, Yvette narrowed her eyes suspiciously. "But you do not even speak English!"

"O but I do!" Jean insisted. Pronouncing the strange words slowly, he said in English, "Hello. My name is John James Audubon. I sail from the France. My place of birth it is the Louisiana. How do you do this day? The weather it is going him that he wore the hat on all of his sorties into Nantes during this final week before his departure.

And there were so many friends to wish goodbye! With the fellows he rambled beside the Loire, fishing in favorite holes, shooting rabbits, watching hawks hunt overhead, spinning grand stories about their feats with girls. But already their boasts and dares were beginning to grow stale in his ears. They kept to the back roads in order to avoid Napoleon's recruiters, who were scouring the countryside for boys just their age. "Won't they catch you when you board the ship?" the fellows wanted to know. "I have my secret means of escape," Jean answered darkly. The secret was nothing more than a false passport, giving his birthplace as Louisiana—a ruse which, together with Papa's friendships among the customs inspectors, should get him safely out of France. But what was the point in spoiling the mystery by telling how his miraculous escape was to be accomplished?

With the girls he strolled in gardens, whispered visions about his brave future in America, and danced, danced! He loved to hook elbows with them and see the look of abandon in their faces and feel their weight tugging at his shoulder as he swung them around, their skirts flying.

One night between quadrilles a flouncy partner named Yvette curled her lips at him, rolled her sly eyes beneath shadowy lashes, and asked, "Aren't you very sad to leave home?"

"Indeed I am," he answered obligingly. He put on an air of brooding melancholy, which he had found to be devastating in

VII
Coueron, August 1803

THERE WAS SO much to do in the last week before his ship sailed for America that Jean fairly danced from place to place. He needed to buy new waistcoats and silk shirts from tailors in Nantes, new boots from the cobbler, new gloves and stockings, new drawing-paper and colors from the stationer's. He had to arrange for the gunsmith to adjust the hammer on his rifle and for the luthier to put fresh strings on his violin. Who knew what the shops would be like in Philadelpha? City of somber Quakers! What would they think of his scarlet waistcoats? As a precaution against appearing too much of a dandy, he bought a Quaker-style hat. It was broad and black and full—as he imagined—of dignity. At home he studied himself in the mirror, and fancied that his green eyes looked mysterious beneath the wide brim. The spectacle so appealed to

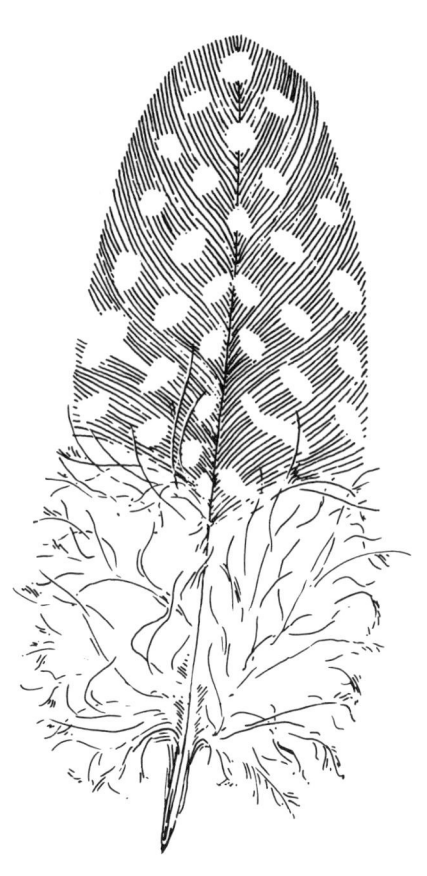

If every drop of blood I have seen were gathered up, the Hudson would not bear it all.

The woods, the woods!

throne, if I am the Dauphin? Why do they hound me for money, always money, if I am the rightful king of France? It is cruel to catch a proud man in the depths of despair and taunt him with royalty.

I remember a monkey and a parrot. The monkey's name was Babu. It had sailed with me from Saint-Domingue. Mother's favorite parrot was named Mignonne. Vile screeching darling. From morning to night it was "Mignonne wants bread and milk!" and "Mignonne is so pretty!" Mother petted the bird more than she petted me. Kill the noisy, mincing thing, I said to Babu. And Babu tore the flimsy cage apart, seized the parrot, and twisted her pretty neck for her. Mother cried and cried. Why, after all these years, do I remember this just now?

You must know these things. I must shovel them out of my heart.

There are not enough bullets in all the world to shoot down every one of the lies.

THE TWILIGHT JOURNAL : VI

I was so tanned and burnt that people mistook me for an Indian. And, in truth, many a day I longed to be an Indian, to walk away from the shop, from town, even from thee and the boys, dear Lucy, from my creditors, from all the stupidities of our race, away into the forest and never look back.

Lucy, my apple, how I wish our flesh were firm again, and we could hang our clothes on the willows and bathe in the Ohio! What occasion have the biddies of Kentucky had to raise their brows over since last they spied us splashing naked in the river? Their scruples will grow stiff from disuse, like old harness dangling untouched on nails in the barn.

I will never see the Pacific ocean. I have tramped and sailed from Labrador to Florida, from Maine to the Yellowstone, but never will I see the Pacific.

Who says I am the Dauphin, son of unlucky Marie Antoinette and Louis XVI? Who says? Who says? Where is my

down his limbs as he struggled into his clothes in the courtyard. Still fastening his buttons, he shuffled quickly away, chased by the sound of their laughter. Ahead, there was no place to go except to the stone house where Papa waited.

hurled helplessly and afraid. She wrapped her arms about him to still his trembling and to guide him. But still he shivered. Unable to bear the intensity of his yearning, he wailed aloud, "Do you love me? Do you? *Do* you?"

"Of course I do," she murmured. "Who wouldn't love such a pretty little sailor?"

The assurance made him cling to her blindly. A numbing twilight washed over his mind. Later, half waking, he was vaguely aware of her escaping from his arms, the rustle of the pallet, the closing of a door.

Later still, he felt a toe in his ribs and blinked up to see her standing over him, dressed once again in the sleazy frock. "That's your two hours," she said, all the warmth gone from her voice. Beside her a thickset man was waiting, arms crossed, cap pulled low over his eyes, shaggy beard fanned out on his chest.

Jean groped for his breeches and began pawing coins from the pocket. "I'll pay for more time," he said.

"Isn't he sweet?" the woman cried gaily.

The man jerked a thumb toward the door and grumbled, "Move it out, boy."

"Just for an hour," Jean begged. "Half an hour!"

The woman tilted back her head and loosed a snort of laughter.

"Get *out!*" the man roared, his beard shaking.

Leaping up, Jean hurriedly grabbed his clothes and his boots, beat the hanging flowers aside with his fist, and dashed from the room. The sudden recollection of failure weighed straw crackling as she patted the coverlet. The jostling of her rounded buttocks seemed to him a deep mystery. He was surprised to see a cross of green stone hanging on a chain between her breasts. Was she a believer, then? Or was the cross mere decoration? The sight of it brought back the memory of his other mamma, the one who had delivered him over to the arms of a sea captain. She also wore a cross of silver between her coffee-colored breasts. Thinking of that vanished mamma, the years fell away from him and he became a child. His hands trembled so badly that he could not undo the buttons on his breeches, and he feared he would cry with frustration.

Coming over to him, unfastening his breeches with deft fingers, her nails like flames against his belly, the woman said, "Have you been a long time at sea?"

"Yes," he lied. "Six months. Away over in the waters of Egypt, fighting the Moors."

"My," she purred, "my, my!" peeling the shirt from his shoulders and the breeches from his trembling legs, "such a pretty young warrior," leading him to the pallet, "such a brave little sailor," drawing him down atop her onto the rustling straw, "so lonely after six months at sea!"

Beneath him, her skin was the color of wet sand. Her breasts and mounded belly and soft thighs were dunes of sand. The cross sliding back and forth on its chain in the valley between her breasts confused him. If she was a believer, why did she spread her legs and take men on this sinful ride? He felt like a quaking leaf, lifted and flung headlong down the wind, strings of his violin. "I'm bound for the South Seas," he added, liking the bold sound of the phrase.

"Such a long way!" She gave him a crooked smile, showing her teeth, and he noticed how her lips gleamed in the lantern light. "A young beauty like you, going home to an empty bunk?" she said. With negligent fingers she reached up and twirled the wisps of hair at the back of her neck. The motion set her heavy breasts to stirring under the thin cloth of her frock. "Wouldn't you like some cheer before you go to the South Seas?"

Gaping at her, cheeks aflame, Jean felt buoyed up and dragged along by an overpowering current, as he had felt once on the Loire when he tried to ride the river in a paddle boat during flood. "Yes," he heard himself stammering as he followed her back through the archway into an inner courtyard. "Yes, I'd like company."

In a small room where flowers were suspended to dry from the low rafters, she told him the price of an hour's pleasure. Shaking with guilt and desire he dug coins from his pocket and counted twice the amount onto the candle stand. "Two hours," he said thickly.

"Two hours for the pretty sailor!" she cooed. In a single sweep of gauzy cloth she pulled the frock over her head and stood naked in the candle light. Swirled by her movements, the air smelled delicately of the drying flowers.

Too shy to look straight at her, Jean turned aside and fumbled at his own clothing, glancing over his shoulder to watch her smooth the bedding on the pallet. He could hear the spent aloft in those jungles of rope. On and on he walked, through broad avenues and crooked side streets, past creaking wagons making nightly deliveries, past knots of staggering sailors, hour after hour until the only lamps burning were those in the bars and brothels.

Outside a grog shop he drew to a halt and gazed longingly in through the brightly lit doorway. Inside, men with arms thrown around one another's shoulders were swaying from side to side in rhythm with their raucous singing. There was a sweet smell on the air. Why not go in? Sing with them, play a fiddle if there was one about, drink whatever it was that smelled so sweet. I can't fall any lower in Papa's eyes, he thought. But a fear came over him that some of his classmates might be in there, celebrating the end of term, and he hung back.

Just then a sugary voice called to him from behind, "Hey there, my beauty! Are you looking for company?"

Turning, he saw on the far side of the street a woman in an archway beneath a hanging lamp. She stood barefoot in a dress of cheap gauzy cloth, her legs spread apart, hands on hips, and gave him a mocking stare. Her tongue flicked across her lips. It was impossible for him to tell from a hasty glance at her painted face how old she was.

He knew he should flee, but a fierce compulsion in his blood pinned him to the pavement and made him reply awkwardly, "I'm on the way to my ship."

"To your ship, is it? All by your lonesome?"

When she spoke, his body seemed to quiver like the taut

down to the three dots symbolizing the triple ideals of the Republic, Jean signed his name on the cover of the exam. Quickly, before the other boys could ask how he had fared, he delivered the pages to the proctor and rushed outside into the crisp evening air. The voices of friends called after him excitedly, but he only hastened his flight. Where to? Not home to Papa. That was all he knew for certain as he stretched his cramped legs: he was too humiliated, too bewildered to face Papa.

Without consciously choosing a direction, he paced along the Charente until he came to a marsh, one of his favorite spots for idling, beyond sight of the town. Startled by his coming, a heron exploded from its roost atop a willow. In the air above the river, swallows were feeding, inscribing perfect arcs on the sky with each dive. Cranes grazing in the shallows folded and unfolded their long legs. With a fussy chatter ducks cruised among the reeds, now and again tipping forward to thrust their heads into the water. How oblivious they looked, how serene! Watching them, Jean forgot for minutes at a time the humiliating exam. But as the red of the sunset leached out of the sky and the birds vanished into hiding for the night, the sense of failure nearly suffocated him once more.

It was quite dark when he reached the first paving stones of Rochefort. Twice he stole past his own house, where he could see Papa at the dining table reading in the glow of a lantern. Unwilling to go in, Jean kept walking. At the harbor, eyes useless in the dark, he listened to wind hiss through rigging on the anchored ships, and he recalled the hours of torture he had barely sit still in his chair. The frenzy to escape reminded him of the time, not long after his arrival at Rochefort, when he had been ordered to stay after class and work by himself on a wickedly hard set of mathematical problems. As soon as he was left alone in the room that afternoon, he slipped out through an open window. He was meandering through the commandant's garden, sniffing roses, when a corporal arrested him for desertion. Eleven years old, larking among the roses—and he was arrested for desertion! Pistol drawn, the officer marched him to the jail boat in the harbor and locked him in with the vermin and riffraff of the port. Vile, vile. Drunks vomiting, lechers pawing, murderers and thieves giving him the eye. Two dozen men in a room no larger than a kitchen, low ceiling, single tiny window, the stench so thick it made him choke. Papa was away then on a cruise, and could not free him. For three days they kept him in that foul pit. "Pretty boy, such a pretty boy," some of the men grunted. He curled himself into a ball on the slimy floor and tried to fend off the coarse words and hands. He was afraid to eat the rank-smelling food, and only drank the water in order to ease the cramps in his stomach. When Papa sailed back into port, he attended to other business for several hours before releasing Jean from the brig. "That is a hotel you will not soon forget, my boy!" Papa declared with a deep laugh when Jean came stumbling, bent over and filthy, into the dazzling daylight. Not soon, Papa, not very soon.

"Time, gentlemen!" the proctor crowed. The grandfather clock hammered its bell.

With the same ornate flourish that Papa always used, right

nervously on the table, tying imaginary ropes. No cadet was better than he at knots or sails, none rivaled him in the use of pistol and sword. But the lowliest one here outstripped him in book knowledge. After three reluctant years of study, he felt more ignorant of ships and tides and mathematics than when he had begun.

He glared at the hunched profiles of his classmates. They scribbled their answers industriously, the burrowing moles. How had he gotten trapped in the company of these brawling, brainy louts, anyway? Let them all become captains, he didn't care. Let them all sail to Egypt and join Napoleon. Let them battle the Turks and the English and the Portuguese. Let them fire their cannons and shout their orders and gain their glory. He didn't care one fig. He would inherit Papa's wealth and buy a hot air balloon, just like the one he had seen lifting a wicker basket from the spot in the place de Viarme where the guillotine used to stand. He would grow rich at some trade (But what trade? He had no least notion.) and buy the gaudiest silk balloon in all of France and travel through the air like a bird. To the South Seas! To America! Outvoyaging Captain Cook!

"One hour remaining, gentlemen, one hour."

He gave up all notion of passing. What was the use of struggling? He might as well have been a butterfly stuck on a pin, fancying he could still fly. Impatiently he festooned the border of his examination with flowering vines. Now he wanted only to escape, to run away and hide from his classmates, and from Papa.

Charged to the brim with desire, baffled, restless, he could

"Of course, sir." Grasping the pencil, Jean hurriedly scrawled a string of numbers across the blank sheet. The proctor gave them a skeptical look, then resumed his clockwork pacing.

Left to himself again, Jean allowed his pencil to drift from the fantastic equations into a sketch of the proctor. Parrot nose, topknot of sandy hair like a feathered crest. For the first time in years he remembered the caged parrots he had been forced to leave behind when his mamma on Saint-Domingue spirited him away from the big house and delivered him over to the strong-armed sea captain. Now they would not be able to spirit him away. Now he would smash the captain right in those crooked teeth beneath the knife-handle moustache, scratch him and kick him and leap from the dinghy and swim to shore. He would rub his skin with ashes and search out the escaped slaves in the jungle and live like a native. Suddenly filled with boldness by these imaginings, Jean stabbed his pencil through the sketch of the proctor.

"Two hours remaining, gentlemen," the proctor intoned from beside the whirring clock.

A feeling of panic gripped Jean once more. He must *do* something. Find some answers, any answers, quickly. He ran his eyes over the printed questions. Shoals, tides, submerged rocks. Square footage of jigger staysails and fore upper topgallants. Furling for hurricanes. Wrecks. His panic and incomprehension chased one another in circles like two mad dogs. All he could see now when he closed his eyes were the patterns of knots. Clove hitch. Sheepshank. Thief's knot. Cat's paw. Bowline with a bight. So many elegant knots. He moved his fingers consuming hatred. Why was he alone in the dark? There must have been a defect in his mind, some blankness that no amount of studying would ever fill.

If he failed, Papa would roar with disappointment. "You do it merely to spite me!" That was what Papa had cried when Jean grew seasick on the very first training voyage. "You are an Audubon, the son and grandson and great-grandson of sailors, and you get sick on ships! Do you enjoy bringing shame on me?" Papa had coughed with anger, and for a long time could not stop coughing. Salt in his lungs. Years in English prisons. Damp stone pits, mold on the wall, rats scrabbling over his legs at night.

And if I fail, Jean thought, doubtless *Maman* would coo with delight. She held a bitter grudge against the sea. "It is nothing but a thief of men," she had told him, "and a source of grief for women. What is the sea but a field for wars and a roadway for deserters?" One day, in the midst of cursing the sea, *Maman* suddenly caught Jean in her arms and murmured, "But without ships and farflung islands and the wanderings of husbands I would not have you, would I, my precious flower?"

A shift in the music of clock and footsteps startled Jean out of his desolate revery, and he looked up to see the proctor standing over him. "Did you by any chance not hear the instruction to begin, Audubon?" the man inquired satirically.

Seen from below, the proctor's flared nose made Jean think of parrots. "Yes sir. I was just thinking, sir."

"Kindly leave some record of your thoughts on paper so that the examiners may judge of your knowledge."

scanned down the examination in a panicky rush. But it was all gibberish. Just as he had feared beforehand, he understood nothing.

Jean glanced in alarm at the other cadets, to see if they were equally mystified. Some few boys were chewing the tips of their pencils, or mouthing words as they read, but most were busily writing out their answers.

The grandfather clock wagged its long brass tail, tick tock, and the proctor with eyes alert for cheaters paced back and forth at the head of the room, hands tucked beneath the tails of his coat, heels clicking in rhythm with the pendulum.

Jean stared hopelessly at his exam. The numbers seemed to rise up off the page and swarm like bees in the air. He started an equation, drawing each symbol with care, but soon he became lost in a snarl of uncertainty. Perhaps if he shut his eyes the textbook diagrams would come back to him, and he could use them to fumble his way toward answers. As if summoned, the crystalline figures from Euclid's *Elements* rose in him like mysterious moons. Spheres, cubes, pyramids, a whole family of polyhedrons, lovely shapes, the building blocks of the universe. Lovely and pure enough to be placed on the empty altars of cathedrals. He believed in them, yet he could not have given a mathematical proof of their existence if his life depended on it. And they yielded him no clue to the problems on the exam.

With eyes shut, despairing, Jean listened to the pendulum of the clock, the footsteps of the proctor, the scratch of pencils. The other boys knew what they were doing. Scratch, scratch, like mice building nests in the walls. He hated them with a

VI
Rochefort, September 1799

AS THE GRANDFATHER clock at the front of the study hall cocked its hammer to strike, the beak-nosed proctor announced in a magisterial voice, "Gentlemen, you will please begin," and all over the room cadets broke the wax seals on their final examinations.

With a sense of foreboding, Jean unfolded the sheet of problems. If he passed, the Navy would put him on the sea for years and years. If he failed, Papa would despise him forever. He struggled to read the first question: *Suppose the soundings in a channel are such-and-such, and the current runs at so many degrees from somewhere-or-other, and your ship draws thus many feet of water, how do you proceed in the event of a cross-wind measuring buzz buzz buzz....* Was this French? The words sounded foreign. He tackled the question again, but could make even less sense of it on the second reading. He tried the next problem, then the one after and the one after, then *know of nature, those jackals, who have never stirred from their arm-chairs? Behold the crude paintings they foist on the public! My own sons, while still in short pants, could paint better rabbits and turkeys.*

⚜

Audubon lies! they say. Audubon invents! What of it? What if I have embroidered my travels with high adventures, with brigands and beauties? Would you prefer dull reality? My memory is not faulty; it is fanciful. The mere fact is no more true to experience than is a dead bird: the fact, like the carcass, must be animated by imagination.

THE TWILIGHT JOURNAL : V

They all looked upon me as an Original Bear, my sons. And did I not dance for them in their drawing rooms and palaces? Hum your tunes, my ladies, and hum your tunes, my lords, for the wild woodsman of America is here to dance for you! You also must learn to prance, my boys, learn to shuffle your feet and wag your head and roll your eyes for the gentlefolk's amusement.

♣

Does thee remember sending me a plait of thy hair, sweet Lucy, all across the ocean to England, and how I did braid it into a cord for my watch? I must have it still, somewhere, that chain of thy hair. Search it out, my dearest, for I would carry it again in my vest.

♣

My work is a beacon to the ages, a tremendous lighthouse! Captains at sea set their course by the glow of my art! Can you not see it, Papa, away over the edge of your ocean?

♣

Ladies and gentlemen, do not mind the noise of those dogs who bark at me, these critics. *Their whining attacks are mere smoke from a dung hill, and will soon evaporate. What do they* turns of coastlines made him think of the bark of trees. On the map of Europe he saw France surrounded by her enemies. England, Spain, Germany, Austria, Italy. The shape of Italy appealed to him. A lady's boot. Girls in the lanternlit doorways, their legs spread open. There was a French army in Italy, conquering city after city. Papa and the other men spoke of it, and of the commander who led them. "Bonaparte," Papa told him by way of inspiration, "Napoleon Bonaparte. Two years ago he was no more than an officer of artillery, and now look how he has risen to command the mightiest army of France! In this Republic, anything is possible for a man of spirit and discipline."

Listening sullenly to the rasp of Papa's breathing, Jean turned the pages of his geography book. Endless Russia. Mysterious China. Bloody Africa, where Elizabeth had come from. Thinking of Elizabeth, he searched for Saint-Domingue, and eventually found it, a tiny blotch like the pincers of a crab, near the tip of Florida. And Les Cayes? Ah—there. The parrot-filled trees, the chattering monkeys, the humped green hills burst on his memory. He must look elsewhere. Some place comforting. The strange, unpronounceable Indian names of Florida caught his eye, and he followed the coastline of North America, in and out of bays, all the way to Canada, a land stolen from France by the English, then across the unimaginable continent, over mountains which the mapmaker had drawn in the shape of breasts, across the inland seas, along rivers, through the vast blank spaces dotted with pictures of beasts and savages, and when at last his eye reached the western ocean, the Pacific, his face was flushed and his heart was racing.

their barracks, while Jean flew as fast as his weary legs would carry him to his papa's house.

The captain was writing letters at the mahogany table. Jean waited to be acknowledged, listening to the wheeze of Papa's breath and the scratch of the quill. After several minutes, without looking up, Papa said in a dry voice, "I hear you were treated to some extra climbing."

"All I did—"

"I don't care what you did or didn't do," the captain said sharply. "I just hope you have been convinced by this little lesson that you must be serious here. You are entitled to no privileges, and you have no *maman* to run crying to. If you are to become a naval officer—if you are to become anything but a spoiled mamma's boy—you must learn some discipline."

"But, Papa—"

"Enough! Save your ingenuity for your books. And when you are finished with your lessons, I have some letters to the Ministry for you to copy."

In a black, black temper Jean spread his books on the mahogany table. Geography, mathematics, history of the navy. He was aching to yell at Papa that a sailor was the last thing on earth he wanted to be. Ignorant, bow-legged, sun-burned lugs, their nostrils filled with gunsmoke. He would rather die than become one of them and go on the sea! But far from shouting his rebellion, he was afraid even to lift his eyes. For a long while he sat staring gloomily at the embossed covers of his textbooks, undecided which subject he hated least. And then he opened the geography, since the maps gave him pleasure. The twists and through the woods outside the town walls, collecting whatever gleamed out at him with the fire of beauty—pebbles or feathers, teeth or shells—sometimes sketching what he saw, much of the time merely looking. But tonight he decided to stay with the other boys, for fear they would talk about him and stop believing his tale.

Clumped together in a whispering knot, the cabin boys ended up following a group of older cadets out through the gates of the naval station into the district of bistros and brothels. The sounds of fiddles and singing and gay shouts washed from the forbidden places into the street. Jean's legs were still weak and his hands ached, but he kept up with his comrades. From a safe distance behind they mimicked whatever the older boys did, scoffing at a blind man who played the flute for coins, stealing plums from an unattended booth, staring at the girls who leaned invitingly with half-laced blouses in lanternlit doorways. But unlike the older cadets, the cabin boys did not actually pursue the gesturing girls into the houses, nor the boisterous music into the bars.

Seeing the big fellows disappear through doorways, their heads nearly scraping the lintel, Jean felt restless, jittery. There was a stirring in his blood, like the beginning of fever, especially when he looked at the girls silhouetted against the lanternlight, their long-nailed fingers caressing their throats, and it frightened him a little, this hot flame in his blood. He shoved his burning hands in his pockets and tasted his own excitement.

When the clock in the town hall began to chime the hour for study, the other boys ran full tilt back through the gates to stuffed with food, jaws working, they looked up at him quizzically.

Imagining they could detect the shameful stains on his face, Jean put on a bold smile. "Have you left me any food?" he said.

Several hands shoved platters and bowls toward his place and several voices began talking at once. They asked eagerly how many times he had climbed the shrouds, what had he done wrong, how was he feeling, would he tell his father on the mate. At the mention of Jean's papa, known to all the boys as commander of one of the training ships, a silence fell over the table.

"My papa would approve, I'm sure," said Jean. And then, glancing at the surrounding tables to make sure no one but the cabin boys could hear, he added in a conspiratorial voice: "He expects me to become the youngest admiral in the history of the navy. That's why I'm given the extra training." They gaped at him, falling for it, and he was encouraged to embroider on his tale. By the time he was finished, talking breathlessly with his mouth half full of bread, he had turned his punishment into a secret tutoring, the ogre of a mate into a benefactor. "So whenever you see me doing extra lessons or chores, don't take any notice. It's only because," he whispered in a lowered voice, once again casting a suspicious look around the dining room, "great things are expected of me."

When the last crumb of food had been wolfed down, the cabin boys discussed what to do with the hour of freedom they were granted between supper and evening studies. Most evenings, Jean went off by himself along the river meadows or

"I can't, sir," Jean called feebly down.

"What's that?"

"I *can't*, sir."

"Too weak, are you? Son of a lieutenant, but you're too damned weak! As soft as a girl! Mamma's boy! Weak little sissy-pants! Isn't that so?"

"Yes sir."

"What?"

"Yes sir!" Jean bellowed in a rage. Filled with shame, he was glad the other boys were not here to see him, to hear him. He let the tears come, scalding, bitter.

"That's what I thought," yelled the mate. The cruelty had gone out of his voice, and now he sounded almost bored. "Hold still there, and I'll give you a hand." There was a jerking and swaying in the shrouds, and in a few moments the mate grappled Jean about the waist with a meaty arm. "Climb on my back and hold round my neck," said the mate, "and we'll be safe down in two shakes."

Numbly, Jean did as he was told, wrapping his arms about the mate's greasy neck, riding him piggyback as he used to ride the back of some other man, long ago, not his papa, some man he had loved a long time ago. Was it *Grand-père*, on Saint-Domingue?

Staggering on wobbly legs across the gangplank to the dock, Jean heard the mate call after him, "Next time think twice before you give me a saucy look, my scrawny monkey!"

In the refectory the other cabin boys were nearly finished with their supper when he arrived. Twin rows of them, cheeks the grassy ramparts encircling the Arsenal like vast green snakes, the marshlands spreading away along the river to the north. Far to the north *Maman* waited for him in his own house. His own room under the eaves was there ready for him, with all its rich stores of lichen, twigs, moss, nests, eggs.

"Don't think it matters you're the son of a lieutenant!" the mate yelled from the deck.

High above the deck, above the town, dizzily resting on the cool planks, Jean remembered the long carriage ride from Nantes, the violin case beneath his feet, Papa reading with a steady frown, the peasants in the fields, the armed villages. And why couldn't *Maman* and Rosa also move here to live in Papa's house? Why must they be left behind? "Women and war do not mix," was all Papa would say. But the war was far away, in other countries, out on the sea, not here in sleepy Rochefort. Papa just wanted to steal away from *Maman*, Jean was convinced, and to steal me from her as well.

"Come down, damn your insolent eyes, or I'll come up after you and throw you in the river!"

It was cruel, beastly and cruel, all this climbing when the other boys had been set free. Shaking with rage against Papa, against the mate, against the whole filthy navy, Jean dangled his legs over the platform's edge and groped for a foothold on the shrouds. When he grabbed the coarse rope the pain in his hands made him cry aloud. The flame roared through his body and a whiteness came over his mind. His arms and legs plunged through the netting and he snagged himself in the ropes and clung there blindly.

"Come on, damn you, come *on*!" roared the mate.

grabbed a rope with his raw palms. His legs were past aching, numb, mere lengths of wood he must bend and lift. The other boys had been set free for supper, and he alone had been kept behind. "Where do you get that saucy look?" the mate had said to him when all the others were dismissed from the training ship. "Think you're the cock of the walk, do you? Well, we'll see what you're made of."

Now the mate was yelling, "Lively, lively there, you dung beetle!"

This climb up the shrouds was Jean's seventh. He clawed at the ropes, blind with sweat, feet slipping, terrified of falling; he struggled until at last he reached the platform midway up the mast and there he flung himself onto the cool planks.

"All right, back down you come, you shriveled toad!"

Jean pressed himself to the platform, heart hammering. If he stepped back onto those swaying ropes, he would surely fall. Tumble screaming and smash himself on the deck. Then would Papa be satisfied? He imagined Papa standing down below in the stiff captain's uniform, watching him fall and feeling bitterly sad. He imagined falling on Papa and crushing him. The breeze chilled his feverish head. It still felt strange, to have all his curls shorn away. *Maman* would have wept to see him. The handsomest boy in France, shorn like a spring sheep.

"Move, you slimy lizard!"

But Jean could not move. Why should he? The mate would not dare to beat him, surely. And it was so lovely to lie here panting with his cheek against the cool planks and gaze down at the ships rocking in the harbor, the barracks, the cannons and gatehouses, the town rising away from him onto its stony hill,

V
Rochefort, August 1796

"FASTER, *you scrawny monkey, faster!*" the mate bellowed from the deck. Jean climbed the rope netting as swiftly as he could, panting, hands raw with blisters. It had a name, this web of rope. What was it? Shrouds—the main shrouds. Everything on the stinking ship had a name, and the mate expected him to learn what to call every last cord and canvas and mast. The ship swaying at anchor beneath him on the river's gentle current wasn't even called a ship; it was a corvette, like the one Papa commanded, midway between a frigate and a sloop. Shrouds, bobstays, royal backstays, jib halyards, leechlines, mizzen, jeers. The names swirled like blown snow in Jean's memory.

"If you don't haul yourself faster, my fine baboon," shouted the mate, "I'll have you climbing all the evening by moonlight!"

Hot tears burned Jean's cheeks, but he could not wipe them away. He scrambled up the shroud, wincing each time he

drag him. Onto the dung heap, the ash pit! They sink their sharp teeth into him and drag him down, the yapping curs, whose hearts are the size of walnuts. Thee knows, dear Lucy, that I am still a considerable admirer of that great man's great deeds, whatever the curs may snarl.

It was ever my dream, to take in with my eyes the whole continent. America! That was my empire. Who cares for paltry France? Who cares even to conquer Europe, so old, so trampled over, so thoroughly known?

I go to jail in Louisville. Every night, I go to jail in Louisville. Audubon is penniless! they cry. How many years ago? Half a lifetime. And still every night my creditors dance in circles around me, calling for my blood.

THE TWILIGHT JOURNAL : IV

The birds you must nearly always kill if they are to pose for you. Once in a great while a living owl or hawk or other bird of prey will hold motionless upon a stand long enough for the slow work of art. But people! Ah, people, my dear sons, will sit still for hours, and even pay you for putting them through this torture! The ladies will gaze at you with the eyes of calves, and some will invite you to adjust their clothing, and some few will offer to disrobe altogether. If wealth and ease is what you are seeking, if you prefer to keep your feet dry and your belly full, if you wish to be spineless hacks, do not chase after birds. Paint ladies and gentlemen.

Many charges are laid against me. Audubon is mad, they say. What does it matter if I go to dinner in my slippers? What does it matter if, when I return from the woods, for a time I snatch the meat from my plate with greasy fingers?

The world speaks ill of Napoleon, now that he is safely dead. Like a pack of snarling curs, the gossips yap at his memory and drag the hero down. Into the mud and mire they

the gutter, dead from the awful fever. Seeing the bodies, Jean tugged the neatly-arranged kerchief from his neck and pressed it to his mouth.

Jean hushed. Across from him, Rosa sat with her lip caught between her teeth and her fists squeezed between her knees.

Twice they were stopped by Guards with tilting muskets, but each time Papa thrust his head out the window, barked a few words, and the carriage was allowed to proceed. Everyone obeyed Papa, even these fierce-looking men with their gleaming guns. Could the gods themselves possess more power?

The carriage rolled across the plaza in front of the cathedral and Jean saw the notices posted on the doors. Cult of Reason: he had read that one day on the yellowing paper. What on earth did it mean? He thought about the cool interior of the cathedral, where his mother used to take him for early mass before the locking of the doors. Far overhead the stone vaults met in midair, a thicket of shadows, like the rafters over his bed, and on sunny mornings light streamed in, thick with dust, inflaming the saints on their pedestals, the priests at the altar, worshippers in the pews, light so substantial he imagined wrapping his arms and legs about the shaft and climbing up through the high windows into the sky.

The cathedral slipped out of sight. Where had the priests gone when the doors were locked? So little of what grown-ups did made any sense. He felt a new onset of fright, just thinking about all the mysterious doings of grown-ups. He watched the city roll by outside the carriage. The dark wood surrounding the window was like the frame of a picture. Houses of dun-colored stone, slate roofs, wheeling pigeons, chimney pots, spires: picture after picture filled the window. Here and there a wall showed pockmarks from bullets. Here and there someone lay in with fourteen cannon on the enemy's ship. Telling Jean about it afterward, Papa trembled with an unspoken joy. *Le Cerbère*, Papa's ship was called. Cerberus, guarding the gates of Hell. In one of Jean's books there was a scary drawing of the terrible three-headed dog. It was queer, how pictures from books stayed in your mind when the picture of your own papa's face slipped and faded.

Noticing Jean, M. Beuscher touched the point of his three-cornered hat. The surgeon would play some role in the adoption ceremony at the town hall, but Jean could not guess what it might be. Would there be a drawing of blood, perhaps? A carving of initials in the skin? Names burned in the chests of slaves. Letters carved in the gray elephant's skin of a beech tree.

"How is the young pack rat?" M. Beuscher asked in a kindly way. On his forehead there was a scar with the shape of a horse's hoof.

"Very well, sir, thank you," Jean answered.

"Your father tells me you have stuffed your room with nests and dead animals and such things."

"It is true, sir."

"He has turned his bedroom into a museum," Papa observed gruffly.

"I did the same when I was a lad," said M. Beuscher.

"The boy needs no encouragement for his idleness," Papa said.

Maman leaned over, a crinkle of silks, and whispered privately to Jean, "Do not provoke him, my sweet. Tomorrow he will be gone again, and we shall be jolly."

Suddenly the street door was flung open and Papa bellowed their names from the hall. "Come, children, come," he shouted, "let's not spend all day at this!" In his tone they could hear how busy he was, how little time he could spare away from his ship, how anxious he was to sail back into the bay to fight the royalists and the English devils.

In the carriage, *Maman*, looking pinched and bitter, drew Jean down beside her on the seat. Staying close to her was difficult, for her many-layered dress was more slippery than a pile of leaves.

While the carriage bore them toward the town hall, Jean glanced sidelong at Papa, who sat in silent fury on the bench opposite. Rosa cowered in rabbity silence at his side. Sometimes, when Papa was away at sea, or off working for the Revolution in other towns, Jean lost the picture of his face. It was surely a stern face, hard and unyielding, as if cut from stone. No wonder the orders it pronounced made men jump.

Maman cupped Jean's chin in her hands and forced a smile. "If you aren't the handsomest boy in France," she murmured, "I would like to know who is."

"For God's sake, Anne," Papa burst out, "will you stop spoiling the boy? You'll turn him into a peacock yet!"

Maman held her smile, but also held her tongue. As if struck, ears burning with resentment, Jean snapped his head to the side and stared out the window. M. Beuscher, the ship's surgeon who had removed another slug of English lead from Papa's leg last summer, was riding alongside the carriage on a dappled horse. That was a terrible battle, the one last summer, did not know what his papa's friends meant when they spoke of casting out the saints, but it had something to do with the locking of the cathedral doors.

Rosa's eyes grew large. "Have they taken down their statues and thrown them in the river?"

"Don't be a ninny!"

Tears sprang to her eyes and she flinched away from him. A door slammed down below. Papa's furious boots stamped across the tile of the entrance hall and out into the street. The front door boomed shut behind him. Rosa leaned so far over the banister that Jean, afraid, impulsively reached out to grab her about the waist. Her body was very stiff, like wood, with the hardness of fear.

"Don't crush your pretty dress," he said, encircling her with his arms, drawing her away from the banister. Seeing her cry was a torture to him.

She squirmed free and stumbled back a couple of steps over the landing. As soon as she caught her balance, she fluffed her silken skirts and cried, "It *is* lovely, isn't it?" She tilted her face up defiantly. There were rivulets in the white powder on her cheeks. "If I can't be Catherine, then I'll be Muguet. Is there any stupid thing wrong with Muguet?"

"That's a fine name," Jean answered consolingly. *Muguet des bois:* Lily-of-the-valley. It was the nickname their *maman* liked to use. White, white lily, such a pure white beauty, with no smirch of chocolate in her skin. No blood of Africans.

"But I don't care what they put down on the papers," she cried fiercely, "I won't answer to anything except 'Rosa'!"

listening to the quarrelsome voices. Papa was often angry, but *Maman* only seldom, and when she cried out in sharp fury, the children felt as if the walls of the house were shaking around them.

"What name would you choose?" whispered Rosa.

"Fougère," Jean answered without hesitation. It was Elizabeth's name for him. Fougère: Fern. Because of his green eyes, the nursemaid said. The word made him think of forests rollicking with bird-cries and humped green hills bursting with the howls of monkeys. "And you?" he asked.

"Catherine," said Rosa.

The name of their mamma in Saint-Domingue. Jean was surprised that she remembered, for they had not spoken of her for a very long time. "You cannot use Catherine."

"Why not?"

"That is a saint's name."

"So?"

"The filthy old saints have been cast out," he announced scornfully, echoing what he had overheard Papa's friends declare when they met in the parlour with their pipes and bottles to talk about the Revolution.

Rosa gave him a bewildered look. She was so little, she understood nothing. Most of the time she was a terrible pest. But once in a while a certain expression on her face made him want to hug her and stroke her hair and whisper to her that it was all right, everything was all right. "Where? Cast them out where?" she said.

"Away." He gave a dismissive wave of his hand. Truly, he

what names to put down on the papers. Papa says they cannot use our old ones."

"From the island," said Rosa in a hushed voice.

"From Saint-Domingue," Jean agreed. It was rare for Rosa even to mention that vanished place. He used to ask her what she remembered, but she would always end up crying and stamping her feet. In his own memory the island had shattered into a hundred bright pictures. Dancers beside a bonfire, a gold bangle in a woman's ear, parrots roosting in dark trees, the silver cross hanging between his mamma's coffee-colored breasts. Elizabeth rarely said a word about Saint-Domingue. Papa forbade the children ever to speak of the island. Jean understood vaguely that *Maman* felt a bitterness toward the place, and Papa had suffered terrible losses there. "A fortune," Elizabeth confided one evening, "your papa lost a king's fortune. And worse than that, he lost other children." "Others?" Jean demanded. Elizabeth nodded sagely: "Love children, just like you and Rosa." "Lost them how?" When she refused to answer, he said, "Because they weren't adopted? Because they kept their old names?" Elizabeth merely shut her eyes and gave a sad moaning noise.

"Papa says we must have new names if we're to be his children in the eyes of the law," Jean explained to his sister. This puzzled him, about the eyes of the law. He hoped Rosa would not ask him what it meant.

The shouts from the parlour rose in pitch. The children tiptoed across the landing and leaned against the banister,

He replied absently, "And you're pretty as a picture, I'm sure."

"Do you think so? Really and truly? Will the magistrate approve?"

The trembling in her voice suddenly made him feel tender, and now for the first time he looked with genuine interest at her reflection. Little sister in a dress of white lace, hair coiled on top of her head, cheeks ghostly with powder. She appeared so very solemn that he wanted somehow to make her laugh. Facing about, he smiled and proclaimed, "The magistrate will ask you to marry him, if you don't watch out!"

This made her blush as well as laugh with delight, and when she blushed the lovely chocolate color rose in her cheeks. That was the blood of Africans showing in her, Elizabeth always said. And that was why the nursemaid dusted her with so much powder, to hide the lovely darkness in her skin, especially today, when they must go to the town hall for the adoption.

"Have you shown *Maman*?" he said encouragingly.

"She and Papa are quarreling."

Jean knew. He had been listening to their angry voices rising up the stairs from the parlour. "What is it about, can you tell?"

Rosa shrugged. "It is something about our names, I think. But I couldn't understand. I get so frightened when Papa yells."

"Ah," murmured Jean, who sometimes enjoyed being older and wiser than his little sister, "they must be quarreling about

IV
Nantes, March 1794

ONE MOMENT the sole image in the cloudy looking glass on the upstairs landing was his own, smoothing the kerchief at his throat, and the next moment Rosa was floating there in the mirror beside him. He frowned. What a nuisance. She would pester him with questions until they left for the town hall.

"You look just like Papa in your suit," she said.

Turning sideways in order to scrutinize in the glass the fit of his black velvet coat, Jean murmured, "I could wear a bigger size."

Rosa peered hopefully into the mirror. "Do you like my dress?" She drew out the white lace skirts to show him.

Glancing at her reflection, he said, "Nice, very nice." He ran fingers through his hair and noted how the curls fell behind his ears. *Maman* would coo over him.

"You look quite handsome," she said.

THE TWILIGHT JOURNAL : III

You are insatiable. What must I do to please you? Is it high literature you want? Do not hunt for any such graces here. Go up the Hudson and look for them in the pages of Mr. Washington Irving or Mr. James Fenimore Cooper. They will supply you with graces enough. Quit pestering me for what I cannot give.

Do not be alarmed. The watchmen of many towns, seeing me out in the roads and fields before sunrise with the collecting bag slung over my shoulder and a gun in my hands, have thought me a harmless lunatic.

I dream of Papa. He is trapped in a hollow tree. He is paralyzed. I must say a name in order to free him, but I cannot think of it. His lips and tongue are frozen in the act of shaping a letter. D, I think it is. The letter D. Papa's gray beard has been shaved, and his jaw is as pink as a newborn's.

The world has its eye upon me. And why not?

a wine glass in two fingers and spun it delicately around, squinting through it at the candle flame, before sipping.

"Here she comes!" a voice cried.

Jean's chin jerked up and his eye was caught by the gleaming blade, falling, falling, his own heart tightening, the blade plunging down. Thunk. Sound of the wooden spoon whacking his skull. The gentleman's curly head sprang free of a neck that was wrapped round with a dazzling white kerchief, and blood gushed out. A soldier grabbed it by the hair and lifted it up for show. Dogs snarled, fighting for position beneath the scaffold.

Hot juices scalded Jean's throat and the sour lump of bread rose into his mouth. A whine burst from him as he spewed the bitter juices. Roaring, the rough boys cleared back from him, scuffing their heavy boots. Then he tumbled forward, but the sharp pain of his knees and hands smacking the pavement stung him awake, and he crawled madly through the crowd, forcing his way between legs, scrambling over boots and clogs and over mudcaked feet wound in rags, ignoring the kicks, the thumps on his back, until he broke free of the shouting thicket and stood up and ran and ran and blindly ran.

all much older than he was. Some of them he had seen swaggering with their arms full of books to the Academie Polysophique in the rue de Bossuet. Some others he had seen loitering at the docks, throwing stones at gulls. "Death to royalists! Death to royalists!" they were chanting now.

Jean ducked into the confectioner's doorway to let them pass. Perhaps he should ask for a candy, so they would think he had business here. The shopkeeper always let him have whatever he wanted, because *Maman* would always pay. "Please, sir, a ginger swirl," Jean said, but one of the oldest boys, whose jaw was shadowy with beard and whose father was also a sea captain, noticed him there at the counter and grabbed him by the sleeve and tugged him out the door, yelling, "Come on, Audubon! Don't miss the spectacle!"

Terrorstricken, Jean was caught up in the gang of boys, hemmed in by their hard elbows and loud voices, and hustled along the streets to the place de Viarme. They shouldered through the crowd until they reached the very edge of the scaffold. The shouting and the shoving and the stench made him dizzy. He shut his eyes, so as not to see. He thought he would fall, but the press of the older boys held him up. Near his feet dogs were licking the stones.

"Ready!" shouted the boy with the beard-shadowed jaw.

The cry beside his ear shocked Jean into looking up, and in a terrible rush he saw on the block the head of a man who used to eat supper at the Audubon house. A gentleman, a merchant who dealt in ladies' gloves. Jean remembered how the man held using the guillotine, and the sound of the guns could be heard all through the city. That would be very quick. A bullet was quicker than anything. But worst of all was drowning. They tied you up and put you in a dinghy, and set you adrift on the Loire, and when you squirmed to get free, a trap beneath the seat hurled you over the side of the boat. And you sank in the water with your arms tied behind. Drowning! Some of the older boys had gone to watch, had stood right on the bank of the river and seen everything, and Jean had listened to them tell about it. The Loire was pretty well jammed with bodies, they said. Only two weeks ago, while looking for birds' nests in the marsh grass, he had seen a woman float by, face-down, her skirts billowing on the water—it could have been any woman at all, even *Mamanfi* —and ever since then he had been afraid to go near the river.

"Jean! Sweetheart?"

It was *Maman* calling, probably to remind him about doing his sums or practicing the violin. But she never called as though she meant it. There was always a little question in her voice, a slithery softness, like cotton, you could slide away from. Not like his father's clanging iron voice. Papa put hooks in you when he spoke. You stood still and listened. But with *Maman*, if you ran off and pretended not to hear, she never got mad. Keeping to the housefronts, where he could not easily be seen from *Maman*'s window, he strolled down the street, nibbling the other slice of bread. Rosa could ask Cook for her own bread, if she ever came home from playing at dolls.

In front of the confectioner's shop he was overtaken by a gang of rough boys with heavy boots and loud voices. They were

Jean imagined Papa in the red cap of liberty and the trim sea captain's uniform, saw the purple veins broken on his face, the squashed nose, the blue eyes, gray beard, imagined him like a prophet out of the Bible, lifting his arm and making people swear. If the people who still wanted a king said no, would Papa have their heads chopped off? Grown-ups seemed to be angry all the time. It troubled Jean, the way they shouted, the way they talked of death at every meal.

"Look now," said Elizabeth, "why aren't you off doing your lessons, instead of here pestering us?" She was helping Cook set out the finished bread to cool. Thump, thump: a row of round loaves like haycocks. Like brown mountains.

"The master has called off school on account of the troubles," Jean explained.

Elizabeth grumbled. It was a noise like a bucket clunking in a well. "Troubles! If you don't stuff a little learning in that pretty head of yours, you'll have trouble enough when your papa comes home, little sir! Trouble where you sit yourself down!"

"Here, you rascal," said Cook, handing him two steaming slices of buttered bread. "Go find your sister and give her one, and get out from under our feet."

He spread the slick butter with his finger and sat on the stoop eating the first slice, keeping an eye out for more prison wagons. If he saw another one come by, he would dash inside and slam the door. The air was cool but the bread was warm. He tried to picture the barber, M. Quentin, without a head. Would it be a terrible pain, when the blade came down? How long would you feel it? Sometimes they shot people instead of wagon rolled by carrying M. Quentin, his barber. The barber's hands were tied behind him and a rag was stuffed in his mouth. Someone had shaved his head, but the job had been done badly, for there were many cuts on his bluish scalp. Even bald and trussed up like that, it was certainly the barber. Jean could never have mistaken the warty nose or sad jowls. The barber never used to smile at him except at the very end of the haircut, when he would draw a sweet from a pocket in his smock and offer it up with a small grin. And look, here were dozens of people trotting along beside the wagon, shouting and jeering at the poor barber! *"Maman! Maman!"* Jean cried, running into the parlor. "They're going to chop off the head of M. Quentin!" "Nonsense," his mother answered. "It is only the powerful who are punished. No one cares about the opinions of barbers." She would not go to the door for a look, and Jean was afraid to return into the street. Next day he stole past the barbershop, and found it boarded up. There was a black X painted over the boards, the shape of Elizabeth's crossed arms.

Now, with the brutal groan of carts again filling his ears, he renewed his pleas to Elizabeth. "If I find you a dead cat, then will you help me with voodoo?"

Her cheeks trembled when she answered, "I left all that mischief back on the island. It's the Devil's work, Master Jean, no business for a white boy to fool with. And if you don't leave me alone about it, I'll tell your papa when he gets back."

His papa was always gone, away in nearby villages training the militiamen, ordering the churches to melt down their bells for cannon balls, making people swear to uphold the Republic.

hear the wheels. He did not want to think about what the wagons carried, or where they were going.

"What does a scamp like you want with black magic?" said Cook. She tugged a wisp of hair from the corner of her mouth. Her face was dusted white, like his mother's, but with flour instead of with the powder that had a stinging smell.

"I want to travel in my dreams," he answered.

Elizabeth gave him a look of disgruntlement. "To that bloody island, I bet."

"You don't know where I want to go," Jean said. But of course she did know. She always could see right into him, with her eyes as dark as chestnuts.

"If you went back there, my little Fern, even in your dreams, they would cut you up and bake you in a pie."

Cook laughed. "And not a bad end for the rascal, if you ask me. Although he would make a lumpy pie!"

Jean stuck his finger into the pan Cook was holding, licked it, then reached for another daub. But Cook rapped him lightly on the skull with her wooden spoon and he flinched away. Thunk. For a moment the sound filled his head. Then it was squeezed out by the sound of wheels rumbling over cobblestones. He knew there was only one place that so many wagons could be going so early in the morning. The place de Viarme, where he used to play at ball with the other fellows before the scaffold had been put up. There were shouts in the street, but Jean did not let himself look out the window, for fear of seeing in a wagon another familiar face.

One day he had been standing in the street door when a

III
Nantes, November 1793

"IS THERE ANY harm in just trying a little voodoo?"

"I tell you and I tell you, Master Jean, I put all that mumbo jumbo behind me," Elizabeth protested.

"Look," he said, opening a specimen box, "I've collected snakeskin and spiders and frogs. What else do you need?"

"I don't need a single solitary thing, because I won't be messing with it." She crossed her arms on her enormous bosom, making a black X, a shape he had seen on doorways. The mark of royalists. Mark of doom.

They were talking in the kitchen beside the fire while Cook fussed at her baking. She was a loud, huffy-puffy woman, who grumbled at her pots and scolded her spoons. "Where *is* that ladle?" she would say. "Has it stood on its legs and walked off?" The window of the kitchen was open on account of the heat from the baking, and the rumble of wagon wheels on the cobbled street forced them to raise their voices. Jean tried not to

I must tell these affairs here on the page, for I have nearly lost the power of speech. I cannot bear to see the look of Lucy as she patiently waits for me to grope for words. The words are slow to come, if they come at all. Sometimes I can only think of the French or Spanish expression, perhaps the Osage or some other Indian tongue. Only here on the page, where I labor with my steel pen, can I wait long enough for the English words to appear.

This paragraph takes me all afternoon. I break three nibs in my fury.

Well, I thought to myself, if the world is to have rich people in it, why should I not be one of them? Riches would set me free to do only what pleases me: dancing, hunting, fishing, tramping through the woods, singing, playing flute and violin, and keeping company with the ladies.

Mr. Combes the phrenologist examined my skull and found it to be a remarkable match for those of Raphael and Napoleon. Search out the records of his examination. Proof, proof! What Mr. Combes had to say about my propensities and faculties was astounding evidence of the merits of science.

THE TWILIGHT JOURNAL : II

It is a Great Work. No matter what the cost, remember that it is a Great Work. Who counts the cost of the pyramids? Who reckons the expense of wives and sons? Who numbers the bodies of the dead? I do, and that is the bitter truth. Thousands of corpses. A pyramid of corpses.

Lucy, my dearest friend, I am in need of some good new socks. Forward them to me in New Orleans. My old ones are all worn out from wading every day through salt marshes. Salt is the ruin of everything. Do not forget the socks, or I shall be forced to go barefoot like a slave.

The ladies in the streets at this hour are not all respectable. Not pure, no, no, they are far from pure, these ladies. They leave their shoulders bare. Their hips move with the squirm of newly-caught fish. I am always uneasy when walking the streets at this hour. Why do they leave their shoulders bare, if not for touching? Why do they roll up their hair like a nest of bees? Their breasts shine like lanterns.

to the harbor. It was a long way to where the ships docked, past many strangers, through twisting streets. But now he could trace almost the whole distance in his mind. Soon he would be able to sneak down there by himself, carrying his clothes in a bundle. Could Rosa walk all that way if he held her by the hand? She was such a short-legged thing. She would cry and drag on his arm and everyone in the streets would stare at them. It would be easier to take along Babu on his chain. But how sad Mamma would be if he did not bring his little sister. Of course he must take Rosa, even if he had to carry her piggyback. They would set out early, before anyone in the house was awake, before even Elizabeth was awake, and they would run until Rosa grew tired, and then they would walk. When a Guard passed, they would hide in a doorway. Perhaps a wagon would give them a ride, or a man on a horse would lift them up into his saddle. "Please, sir, could my sister and I ride with you as far as the docks? We are sailing today." And at the harbor he would ask to speak with the captain of each ship until he found one that was bound across the ocean to Saint-Domingue. If the captain asked him for money he would offer to work. He was strong. He could coil ropes. He could sweep. If the captain still said no, he would wait until the man turned away and then sneak with Rosa onto the ship, into a dark corner to hide.

Leaning out the window, imagining how it would be, he did not worry about pirates. He did not even care if the ocean made him sick. That kind of sickness would pass.

how you feel. I know just exactly how you feel. Tiny Rosa, she'll forget. But not you, my green Fern, not you."

She drew pictures on his back with her finger and had him guess what they were. Sun—a round ball. Grass hut—a shaggy hump. Bird—two wings and a body like a knife to cut the air. After a while she just drew circles, and sang. It was not a dancing song, not a drumming song, but a song for children in the night time. Fooled into thinking he was asleep, she kissed him on the hair, leaving a smell of bark, and went away.

When all was quiet he rolled over and stared up at the vault of rafters. The candle made them ripple with shadows. Whenever he was left alone to remember, he felt very far away from anywhere and very lost and afraid. He tried to think of stories his father had told him, about pirates and prisons. But he could not stop thinking about things that hurt. Unhappiness made him get out of bed and go to the window to see what there was in the street. He opened the chipped green shutters and looked down. A wagon loaded with barrels. Two Guards with muskets propped on their shoulders. Rats scrabbling over garbage in the gutter. His papa had eaten a rat in prison once. An English prison. The English were devils. They shot Papa in the leg and kept him in a stone room and fed him so little food that he ate a rat. Papa still had the cough they gave him, and the limp. No wonder he sent the English pirates down to the bottom to drown.

By leaning far out the window Jean could see to the corner where he and his papa always turned when they walked down

When the bell in the church down the street rang nine, Jean opened his eyes and saw the captain fishing the gold watch out of his vest pocket.

Before his papa could announce bedtime, Jean wriggled down from the cushiony lap and made his good night bow.

"No kiss?" said his *maman*, pursing her lips.

He whirled about and raced up the stairs, a fast runner, feet scarcely touching the wooden treads. At the top he slammed blindly into Elizabeth, the nursemaid.

"What a rush, little hurricane!" she laughed, grabbing him beneath the arms and lifting him until his eyes were on a level with her own gleaming black face. "So anxious for bed, are you? Or is it Elizabeth's stories? Come, then, and I'll tell you a story about the magic island."

Her island, his island. Saint-Domingue. Elizabeth had been gone from it longer than his whole life, but she remembered more than he did. She remembered everything about that place, even though she had not been born there. She had come from Africa, a bloody country. "About as bloody as this nasty France is right now," she told him once. As soon as he was in his nightshirt, and the room under the eaves was dark except for a single candle, and Elizabeth had begun telling about the island, he saw his real mamma standing at the end of the dock, waving her straw hat as if she were drawing the shapes of the hills in the air. And then he sobbed. He shoved his face into the pillow and sobbed and sobbed.

"Never you mind, little Fern," Elizabeth soothed. "I know

what became of all the sailors?" Jean asked. "Why," said his papa, "what could they do but drown?"

Captain Jean Audubon, that was his papa's name. The many people who came to talk with him about the troubles sometimes called him Citizen Audubon. "We are in need of cannon, Citizen Audubon." "How can we be confident of our neighbors' loyalty, Citizen Audubon?" And when they lifted their glasses for toasts, they cried, "Long live the Republic, Citizen Audubon!" Now that is my name, the boy thought. Jean Jacques Audubon. And little Rosa was Rose Audubon. You must never never answer to the old names again, Papa said. Au-du-bon. Jean shaped the word with his lips, but made no sound.

"There are more cakes on the tray," said his *maman*.

"He's had quite enough," said Captain Audubon. "Do you want him to turn into sugar?"

"He is a sugar already." Her face creased again from a smile, just like his papa's cracked wallet. Like the pattern of rivers on a map. That made her face seem prettier, thinking of maps. She pushed the needlework onto the table and opened her arms in invitation. "Aren't you a sugar, little Jean?"

He climbed dutifully onto her lap, but he would rather have climbed into the pages of his book, to live there with the lions and the foxes. He clung to the book, using it as a shield, and would not lean against her frilly bosom. The arms she wrapped around him were fat and heavy. Her white powder smelled like burned syrup. It stung his nose. He shut his eyes and held his breath and thought about curling up in the hammock on the porch of the big house. In a minute she would let him go.

"Yes, Papa."

"Are you too hot in your jacket?" asked his new *maman*. "You may sit in your shirt if you'd like."

"I am cool enough," he answered, not calling her *Maman*, even though she was begging with her eyes for him to do so.

The pictures were lovely. Lions and foxes and weasels and mice. Ink as black as night. There was even a monkey that looked just like his own Babu. But there were no parrots. "La Fontaine knew nothing of those wild islands," his papa had explained when Jean asked him why there were no parrots. His new *maman* kept two parrots in a cage beside her sewing table. Mignonne, one of them was called, and it scrawked constantly for biscuits. Jean loved parrots, but he despised this begging Mignonne. Every chance he got, he pulled at the bird's feathers. His papa had brought it from Saint-Domingue in a ship.

Thinking about ships gave Jean an ache in the stomach. How long had they sailed, he and Rosa and the monkey? He could not be sure, because he did not quite know the names of his days yet. And all the way across the ocean he had been sick. He could not even eat the captain's chocolate. If feeling that sick had not killed him, how bad would he have to feel in order to die? It was lucky they had met no pirates. His papa had met with pirates many a time, many a time. "But the English privateers are the worst of all," his papa told him. "I carry a little memento of them right inside here," tapping his thigh, "a morsel of English lead."

Once, his papa had battled an English privateer for three hours and sent it right down to the bottom of the sea. "And

II
Nantes, France, July 1791

His new *maman* had an old face. Under the white bonnet, above the white lace collar, behind the white powder it was not the color of coffee beans. It was red, the color of your nose when you had a fever. When she smiled with it, as she was smiling at him now over her needlework, the creases in her skin reminded Jean of his papa's cracked sea-going wallet. From the carved chair at the end of the table his papa was also looking at him, but without smiling, so Jean bent down over his illustrated book. He longed to become invisible. Rosa had already been sent to bed, riding on Elizabeth's fat hip. The pages smelled of vanilla. It was his favorite book, La Fontaine's *Fables*, the one his real mamma used to read to him on the plantation in Saint-Domingue.

"If you keep at your lessons," his papa said, "eventually you will be able to read those words, and not merely look at the pictures. What good is a sea captain if he cannot read?"

My eyes go. The Hudson is a smear of gray water. I cannot see the cliffs on the far side. Stone cliffs. The turkeys and prairie dogs pose in my head, but I can no longer paint them.

And what if I asked to have the heads of Negroes shipped to me in kegs of whiskey? They were dead Negroes, were they not? They were unclaimed corpses, were they not? Buried at the public's expense! Is that cause for shame? Is it? Is it?

I catch Lucy watching me sidelong. In her face, not the patient fury with which she always used to greet my changing moods, but a look rather of forbearance, as if I were a child to be humored. A child!

Bachman comes to protest that my notes for the Yellowstone journey are incoherent, of no use to him in pursuing work on the Quadrupeds. *He asks me about ground squirrels. I do not remember seeing any. Fox? None that I recall. I recollect only buffalo and Blackfeet warriors and the smell of the campfire.*

Later, I hear him whispering to Lucy outside my study, "Dear Audubon's mind is ruined!"

them his adventures. In those lucid moments he also wrote the fragmentary notes that are published for the first time below.
—LUCY BAKEWELL AUDUBON

♣

I, John James Audubon, being of sound mind and body, do herein untangle the snarled tale of my life. I, Jean Jacques Audubon. I, Jean La Forêt Audubon. I, Jean Jacques Fougère. I, Jean Rabine.

I am a bastard.

♣

Lies, lies all about me. A cocoon of lies. I am inside with a knife.

♣

They test me. Lucy asks, do I remember eating dinner with President Sam Houston in Texas. I do not. But I remember drinking too much brandy at her father's house, suffering bruises when my carriage overturned, watching an elephant with frost-bitten ears uncork a whiskey bottle and drink from it. The mind is a warren of caves.

♣

THE TWILIGHT JOURNAL : I

Had I not promised my late husband on his deathbed that I would publish his journals, I would not now be placing these unseemly and at times unsavory memoirs before the eye of the public. He reveals matters in these pages—dark secrets or perhaps dark inventions—which he never confessed to me in person. I have faithfully transcribed every word from his palsied handwriting, neither softening nor deleting, even though certain entries cause me great pain. My only alterations have been in matters of spelling, punctuation, and grammar, arts which my husband, even in his years of vigor, had never fully mastered. Doubtless his many eager detractors will find grounds here for new attacks. So be it. We shall see whose fame survives the century.

The reader should be warned that my husband was not entirely in his right mind when he began these journals, and that he was far indeed from rationality by the time he faltered to a stop. Soon after returning, in 1843, from his expedition to the Yellowstone, he began to lose his faculties, first the steadiness of his hands, then his eyesight, his memory, and eventually sweet reason itself. During those twilight years between 1843 and his death in 1851, he would at times still enjoy moments of lucidity, as on a stormy day the winds will occasionally part the clouds and unveil the sun in all its burning brilliance. For hours at a time he would labor with his old industry at the book on mammals, or dance the grandchildren upon his knee and tell

"Hush, or you'll frighten the little one."

From his *grand-père*'s arms little Rosa looked at him with large eyes, too frightened to cry.

They came to the end of a wharf and a dinghy was waiting there. Four sailors in striped shirts at the oars. A captain all in blue, dark moustache across his lips like the handle of a knife.

"No!" Jean bawled. Then he clamped his mouth shut and began kicking, scratching, flailing his fists. But at the same time he was afraid of hurting Mamma. What he longed to do was touch her throat, kiss her, feel her arms drawn about him like the warm sling of a hammock. He saw *Grand-père* hand the monkey and then Rosa down to the waiting sailors. Then suddenly the captain was reaching up, and his mamma was pushing him away, pushing him away, pushing him away into the captain's huge blue arms, which were strong, the strongest Jean had ever felt, and they crushed him into stillness.

The dinghy rocked as the sailors pulled on the oars. The captain pointed at the three-masted ship and promised, "You can ride in my cabin. You can look through the spyglass, and eat all the chocolate you want."

But Jean twisted around in the captain's fierce arms to stare at the dock, where his mamma stood alone. She lifted the straw hat and waved it from side to side. The shape it made in the air was the same as the shape of the mountains, green humps rising beyond the harbor, beyond the town, all across the only sky he had ever known.

new parrots in France." The shiver in her voice made him let go of the cage and keep still.

Now her ginger-smelling hands stroked his forehead. The touch on his skin made him feel very light, as if he might rise from his mamma's lap and float up into the air with the crying birds.

When he awoke he was riding in her arms. His face was against her throat and he felt the quick pulse on his cheek. The beat of it was frightening, almost as if his mamma herself were afraid. Could she be afraid? There was just enough light for him to see *Grand-père* Gabriel, who must have come to the cane field in the night, walking behind with baby Rosa and the monkey. Jean pretended to sleep, so that his mamma would not make him walk. Even without opening his eyes, he could tell when they reached the harbor, from the smell of cotton and coffee and from the dizzy cries of gulls.

"I won't go on the ship!" he wailed, squirming to get down from her arms.

This only made her squeeze him more tightly, until his breath hurt. She was trembling, and seemed strange. Was this truly Mamma? Or a demon in her body? Beneath the wide straw hat her eyes were red. She carried him past bales of hides, dry whiff of leather, then past sweet kegs of rum, and her arms would not bend.

"Your papa will meet you," she said. "Your new *maman* will take you in. See, there is your ship out in the bay. Such a pretty ship!"

"I don't *want* to go!" he cried.

their arms and the names of their owners burned in their chests. On their backs they had pale pink stripes from the whips. Sometimes a dancer would pick him up and swing him around until all the world was spinning. Then one of the servants from the big house would carry him, dizzy, home to bed.

These days Jean was afraid to go anywhere near the slave huts, even if his mamma would let him. At the big house the older children had been saying that all over the island the slaves were butchering the planter families. Cutting them up and trailing their guts on the ground. Hacking the bossmen into pieces and chopping off the legs of their sons and daughters and burning their houses. That was what the older children had been saying. One night Jean stood in a circle of listeners surrounding a new boy, a husky thin-lipped fellow whose family had just moved into the big house, and heard him say:

"At our place they stuck a white baby on a spear and carried him past the windows, with him still kicking and bawling, and then they cooked him over a fire on the lawn where we could see."

Remembering this in the ditch, Jean struggled to keep his eyes open. Overhead the black shapes of night birds sliced the air, delivering dreams. In the daytime the swooping birds were like scraps of fire, blazing reds and greens and blues. In a cage of twigs beside his bed there were two parrots. When his mamma rushed in this evening to gather him up along with his sister, she agreed to bring the monkey, but she would not bring the birdcage. "We must hurry, child," she told him. "You will get he had ever known was this one who squeezed him now with strong arms in the wet ditch of a cane field.

Yesterday she had said to him, "You will sail across the ocean to France, dear green-eyed Jean, and there you will meet your papa, and you will have a new *maman*."

"I won't go!" the boy cried.

"You must go, child. Here it is not safe for a little white-skin like you."

The boy could not remember his father. A sea captain, they told him. Owner of many slaves. A trader in sugar and rum. Rich, rich. But the boy always grew sick in boats and he did not care about money. Nor did he have any desire for a new *maman*. He would not go on the ship. If the big house was dangerous, he would hide here in the cane field with his second mamma and his pet monkey and his whimpering sister, silly Rosa, only four years old, but he would not go on the ship to France. He was six, a fast runner, quick with his mind, able to look after himself.

Wind rattled the stalks of cane. Soon the monkey grew still in his arms, and Rosa quit her whimpering.

"Sleep, my green eyes, sleep," his mamma whispered. "In the morning the ship will come for you."

But fear kept Jean awake. The drumbeats and the voices coming from the slave huts sounded angry. What made them so mad? Long ago, before the anger, he used to go down from the big house to the slave clearing and listen to the drums and watch the dancing. The women wore great shiny earrings. Their skirts bloomed with flowers. The men had tattoos on

I
Les Cayes, Saint-Domingue, June 1791

NIGHT BIRDS were screaming in the trees. Monkeys were howling in the black humps of hills. Scraps of darkness shook loose from the branches and glided away. Dreams, the boy thought. Dreams flying out to visit sleepers, if there were any sleepers on this night of bonfires and drums. The boy longed to be home sleeping in the big house, not out here in the field of sugar cane hiding in a wet ditch. He had never stayed up this late before.

"See the dreams flying," he whispered to his mamma, pointing at the black shapes overhead.

"Hush, sweet," his mamma whispered back, and put her hand over his mouth, and squeezed him against her. She was strong, strong enough to carry the boy and his sister and his pet monkey all in her arms at once. Her skin smelled of ginger. In the daylight it was the color of coffee beans. Really she was his second mamma. His first was in heaven. But the only mamma

Copyright ©1984 by Ursula Le Guin and Scott R. Sanders.
All rights reserved.
Printed in the United States of America.

Gratitude to the National Endowment for the Arts for their valuable assistance.

LIBRARY OF CONGRESS CATALOGING IN PUBLICATION DATA
Le Guin, Ursula K., 1929
THE VISIONARY.
No collective t.p. Titles transcribed from individual title pages.
Texts bound together back to back and inverted.
1. American fiction—20th century.
2. Audubon, John James, 1785-1851—Fiction.
I. Sanders, Scott R. (Scott Russell), 1945- . Wonders Hidden. 1984.
II. Title.   III. Title: Wonders hidden.
PS659.L4   1984   813'.54'08   84-7656
ISBN 0-88496-219-9 (pbk.)

PUBLISHED BY
Capra Press
Post Office Box 2068
Santa Barbara, California 93120

SCOTT R. SANDERS

Wonders Hidden:
Audubon's Early Years

CAPRA PRESS
1984